I0603068

About The Author

Discovering a passion for storytelling early in life, at twenty-one years of age Kate published her debut novel The Wilted Rose, a novel inspired by the true story of a Brisbane family's experience with mental illness during the 1960s. This book was the beginning of a passion for Creative Nonfiction. Kate has since gone on to publish three more books and multiple short stories across various genres.

Kate has received recognition from writing awards and competitions around Australia. The Hunter Writers Centre in Newcastle consecutively selected Kate's entries to the Grieve Writing Competition two years in a row, for publication in the competition's annual anthology. One of these entries was also chosen for the inaugural Hunter Writers Centre Award. Kate has also been a finalist in the Reader's Digest 100 Word Short Story Competition.

Kate is currently working on a sequel to The Wilted Rose, and an Irish Noir novella series set in Galway.

In her writing, Kate takes a particular interest in exploring various human experiences and perspectives, using her writing to help to share people's stories in the wider community.

The Wilted Rose

Kate Kelsen

Pineapple Publishing

CONTENTS

Part One:
The Rose Bud

Chapter One

Maleny, Queensland, Australia
1946

Sitting on the ledge by her bedroom window, Sarah looked out over the landscape that surrounded her home. The earth was dulled by the shadows of the lingering night, and the colour of sunrise burst through over the mountains into the misty grey.

A barbed-wire fence divided her family's property from the dairy farm next door, which her father Phillip managed for the owner. Just beyond the prickly fence stood the milking shed, a sturdy timber building that had withstood the harsh Australian sun and many wild summer thunderstorms over the years.

Behind the house and farm the land fell away into a valley, and Sarah smiled as she watched four dairy cows plod their way up the path, heading for the milking shed. Charlie the cattle dog nipped at their ankles, barking and darting this way and that.

Not far behind was Sarah's father, wrapped in a weathered trench coat and gumboots, using a crooked stick to pull himself up the hill. Each morning Sarah's brother Ron helped him round up the cows for milking. When Ron left his father, he brought the first bucket of milk up to the house for breakfast. Just thinking about it, Sarah could taste the delicious porridge with fresh cream and milk straight from the cow.

Life on the land was sweltering hot in summer and freezing cold in winter. A flower garden provided a colourful and fragrant oasis close to the house. Amongst the other plants, trees and bushes, a rose bush was situated beneath Sarah's bedroom window, and she could see a fresh bud still hidden amongst the leaves. She could hardly wait to see it in full bloom.

Sarah slid off the ledge by the window and crossed the room.

'Vivienne,' she whispered, crouching beside the bed and gently shaking her little sister.

Vivienne groaned, stretching out from underneath the covers.

'Come on, you,' Sarah chuckled. 'Up you get.'

The aroma of oats wafted down the hallway as the sleepy-eyed siblings shuffled their way to the kitchen table. Their mother Aileen stirred porridge in a large cast-iron pot over the wood-fired stove. She spooned a helping into five bowls, passing them along to each of her children. She took her seat at the table, clasping her hands together as she bowed her head and closed her eyes. The children did the same, sitting quietly as Aileen's words rolled off her Scottish tongue.

'God, we thank ye for yer goodness, and yer kindness, and for this food we thank ye now. Amen.'

After they had scraped their bowls clean, Aileen fetched the big black leather Bible from a nearby side table, dropping it in front of Ron with a commanding thud. She opened the book to the page marked with a thin ribbon.

'Alright Ron, please lead us in the mornin' readin'.'

Ron was the only son in the family, so when his father was not there, he was the man of the house. Dodging yawns as he read, he perked up in the process of sounding through Old English text. Sarah and Vivienne listened diligently to their brother, while Aileen hissed at Hilary and Bridget to sit up and pay attention.

The bounce of Ron's young voice paid no tribute to the weight of the message being read, bringing an innocent touch to the difficult content. He finished the passage and looked up at Aileen with a beaming smile. He was very proud of himself and his efforts.

'Very good Ron. Very good.' Aileen nodded. 'I am so pleased ter hear ye readin' from the Bible. Now let's bow our heads in prayer.'

Having finished milking the cows for the morning, Phillip arrived back at the house for his breakfast.

'Aileen, the buckets are in the drip safe ready for the butter.'

'Thank you, love. I'll go and start churning. Sarah, ye can come out and help me after ye and the others have done the dishes.'

The drip safe was a frame covered in hessian bags, stored on the back veranda. Sarah dripped water over the hessian to keep it cool and save the milk from spoiling. She thoroughly enjoyed patting the butter, using special paddles similar to table tennis bats to keep the slab of butter moving from one paddle to the next until no more moisture could be seen.

Once they had completed their morning chores, Sarah, Vivienne and Ron prepared for school. Standing before her bedroom mirror, Sarah brushed her hands over her uniform blouse and skirt, and then used pins to secure her waves of thick brown hair back off her face. Her glasses were oval shaped with fashionable pointed flecks in the top outer corners. She pushed them up the bridge of her nose, regarding her reflection once more.

With their hessian satchels over their shoulders, Ron, Vivienne and Sarah left for school. With Bridget and Hilary by her side, Aileen saw them out the door. The school was a twenty-minute walk down the dirt road. As they passed the dairy farm and approached the property that bordered on the other side, Sarah spotted old Mr. Gibson, their neighbour and friend of their father. Mr. Gibson was attempting to approach a lean dark horse, but the skittish animal shied, backed away and bolted every time he got close.

More children from the neighbourhood joined their group as they walked along. They arrived in the Maleny township and split up as they entered the schoolyard.

'Ron, don't forget I have netball practice this afternoon,' Sarah called. 'You'll be walking Vivienne home on your own!'

'Okay,' Ron responded, waving back at her.

Between classes, Sarah attended school committee meetings and spent lunch breaks with her friends. That afternoon the bell clanged, signalling the end of the school day. Sarah walked to the oval on the edge of the school grounds with her teammates. Their coach, Mrs. O'Connell, split the girls into two groups, one side acting as defence and the other as offense.

'Sarah, will you captain the defence team for me?' Mrs. O'Connell requested.

'Yes, Miss,' replied an excited Sarah. This was the first time she had been asked to captain a side.

Sarah organised her teammates into the positions they would play. They were determined to win this time. Their goalie shot the winning goal.

Mrs. O'Connell blew her whistle, and Sarah's team jumped up and down triumphantly. They were delighted that they had worked so well as a team.

Walking home after practice, Sarah again spotted Mr. Gibson in his paddock.

'G'day, Sarah.'

'Hello, Mr. Gibson,' Sarah replied, approaching the fence.

'How's life been treatin' you then?'

'Good, thanks.'

'Been at netball practice this arvo?'

'Yes,' Sarah replied.

She dropped her bag and lent against the fence.

'What is that horse's name, Mr. Gibson?'

'Dawn,' he groaned.

'I walk past here every morning and afternoon and I just can't help but watch her. She is so beautiful.'

'Ha!' Mr. Gibson scoffed. 'Beautiful is the last word I'd use to describe her. Such a fiery nature that one, I can't get near her. Got her from another farmer a while ago. Dunno what caused the bad temper. Lack of discipline, I'd say.'

'I still think she's beautiful,' Sarah sighed, resting her chin on her folded arms.

'I've been tryin' to break her in for months,' Mr. Gibson continued. 'I'm starting to doubt I'll ever have any luck.'

Sarah lifted her head. 'I'd like to try.'

'Ha!' Mr. Gibson teased. 'How old are you, eleven?'

'Yes, I am. But I know I'd be safe if you helped me. I'd really like to try if you'd let me.'

'I like your spirit, girl.' Mr. Gibson sighed loudly in submission. 'Okay, how does this sound? If you believe that horse is meant for you, you can have her, if you can ride her. And that's only with you father's say so.'

'Really, Mr. Gibson?'

'Really.'

'Oh, Mr. Gibson, thank you!' Sarah squealed, picking up her bag. 'I can't wait to tell my parents! I'm so excited!'

'Come by in the afternoons and we'll spend some time with 'er and see how she likes you.'

Sarah snatched up her bag and took off toward home. She still had her afternoon chores to do, and her mother would be upset if she was delayed any longer.

'I'll see you tomorrow, Mr. Gibson!' she called over her shoulder.

'Alright then,' Mr. Gibson chuckled.

Chapter Two

'A horse.'

'Yes, Father. Mr. Gibson said he would help me break Dawn in. He offered to teach me to ride. And I have had some practice before.'

Phillip raised his eyebrows in thought.

'Well, I suppose you are old enough to start riding,' he agreed. 'But a horse is a big responsibility, Sarah. You have to ride, feed and groom them every day.'

'I'll ride Dawn to school,' Sarah insisted. 'My friends ride their horses and check on them at lunchtime. There's a special yard to keep them where they can run around.'

'Alright,' Phillip agreed. 'I will come to Mr. Gibson's farm when the horse is ready and see for myself that you can ride her.'

'Oh, thank you, Father!' Sarah squealed, clapping her hands together. 'Thank-you so much! I promise I won't let you down, I promise!'

The following afternoon, Sarah followed Mr. Gibson into his paddock.

'Now, what I want you to do first is just approach her slowly. Don't make any sudden moves or loud noises. If she gets startled, pull away. We don't want you gettin' hurt.'

Sarah took a few steps forward, her heart thumping in her chest. She could see Dawn watching her out of the corner of her eye. Dawn turned her head, tossed her mane and snorted. Sarah stood still for a moment, and then crept forward again, slowly raising her hand. Dawn jerked and backed away.

'Be careful, Sarah,' Mr. Gibson warned.

Dawn twitched her ears, and Sarah reached out and stroked her muzzle, speaking softly.

'It's alright. It's alright.' She looked into Dawn's gentle dark eyes. 'I will take care of you. I promise. I will never ever hurt you.'

The more time Sarah spent with Dawn, the gentler Dawn became. Every afternoon after school Sarah diligently showed up to Mr. Gibson's farm, and she and Mr. Gibson spent time walking her around the yard on a rope, gently talking to her all the while. One day, Mr. Gibson suggested they try to fit Dawn with a saddle and bridle.

Sarah checked that the girth of the saddle was strapped tight under Dawn's belly. She slipped her foot into the stirrup, placing her left hand on the saddle and her right on the bridle. She lifted herself up, and Dawn jerked, sending Sarah stumbling backwards. Mr. Gibson jumped forward to grab her.

'Are you right?' he asked, concerned.

'Yes, I'm fine,' Sarah replied.

She stayed back a moment, gathered herself and repositioned her hands, pulling herself up again. She carefully swung her leg over Dawn's back. Dawn staggered on her feet as Sarah settled into the saddle. When they were ready, Mr. Gibson slowly guided them into a walk. Without warning Dawn reared up on her hind legs.

'Whoa, Dawn, whoa!' Mr. Gibson cried, struggling against Dawn's strength.

Sarah held on tight, slipping backward in the saddle.

'Whoa, Dawn! Whoa!' Mr. Gibson pulled on the reigns, and Dawn dropped back down onto all four legs again.

'Are you right, Sarah?'

'Yes.' Sarah closed her eyes, nodding, breathing. 'Yes. I'm fine.'

Mr. Gibson led Dawn into a walk again, taking her in circles around the paddock. Sarah leaned down and stroked Dawn's mane.

'You're doing well, Sarah,' Mr. Gibson reassured her. 'I still can't believe we're doing this.'

When Mr. Gibson deemed Sarah ready, Phillip accompanied

his daughter to the farm. Mr. Gibson greeted them as they approached the front gate, and the men firmly shook hands.

Phillip leaned back against the fence, his arms tightly crossed as he watched Sarah with Dawn. Sarah guided Dawn into a walk, then a canter, and then a gallop. The men watched as she rode unaided around the paddock.

'It's a miracle!' Mr. Gibson laughed, shaking his head. 'It's unbelievable! No-one else has been able to get on that horse!'

Sarah pulled Dawn up before them. 'I did it!'

'Well, I never thought I'd see the day,' Mr. Gibson confessed. 'Like I said, she's all yours. If you can do what I just saw you do, you deserve her. Well done.'

'Thank you so much, Mr. Gibson,' Sarah grinned. 'I'll take good care of her, I promise.'

'I know you will.'

Sarah stepped down to the ground, and Mr. Gibson looked from her to Phillip.

'You got a very clever daughter here, Phil,' he assured.

Phillip nodded.

'Thank-you, Tom. I know.'

Sarah upheld her promise to her father and rode Dawn every day, except for Sundays. Dawn was an animal in Sarah's care, and the responsibility filled her with a sense of love and compassion that she had never experienced before, different to what she felt for her family. She loved Dawn with all her heart, possibly even more than she loved herself.

After helping to clean up after Sunday lunch, Sarah carried a square bale of hay and a tin bucket of brushes into the paddock. She tossed a biscuit of hay onto the ground, and Dawn abandoned the grass she was ripping out of the ground in favour of the hay. Sarah took a brush from the bucket and loosened stiff dirt and dust from Dawn's coat.

As the sun began to fade Sarah sat on the fence and watched Dawn mosey around, tossing her mane and flicking her tail. Sunday was the only day that she was not allowed to ride, but that single day felt like an eternity. She yearned to ride with Dawn through the fields, free as the wind.

Sarah reached her hand out, and Dawn raised her head to it. The air grew cool, and as she fitted Dawn with her night blanket, her mother's voice bellowed across the property.

'Sarah, come on up here now! It's time ter get ready fer church!'

She turned and saw her mother standing on the back steps of the house waving at her.

'Alright,' she called. She turned back to Dawn, stroking her muzzle. 'I've got to go now, but I'll be back in the morning.'

'Sarah! Hurry! We'll be late!'

Chapter Three

After netball practice, as the girls gathered their satchels Mrs. O'Connell called to Sarah.

'Will you stay a minute, Sarah? I'd like to talk to you about something.'

Sarah said goodbye to her friends and turned back to her coach.

'I have a proposition for you, Sarah. I would like to make you team captain.'

Sarah raised her eyebrows. 'Really?'

'I know you can do it. It is a big responsibility, but I believe in you. You work so well with the other girls and are a true leader. You played well today, as you do every day. So, what do you say?'

'I would love to be Captain!'

'I would be honoured! Thank you, Mrs. O'Connell!'

'I'd hoped you'd say that. I know you can do it.'

Amidst Sarah's excitement, a burning sense of determination sent the spring into Sarah's step as she headed for home. She could hardly wait to tell her family her news.

'Mother, Father!' she cried as she skipped into the house.

Aileen was in the kitchen cooking dinner. She followed Sarah into the living room, where Phillip was reading the newspaper. He looked up at Sarah, Aileen standing behind her.

'Mrs. O'Connell has asked me to become the team captain!'

'Oh, Sarah, that's amazing!' Phillip exclaimed.

'She wants me to start right away! On Sunday!'

Phillip tensed his brows.

'On Sunday?'

'Yes, that's when the competitions are held. But it is always in the afternoons, so I can still go to church in the morning.'

Phillip sighed, shaking his head.

'You can't play on Sundays, Sarah. You know this.'

'Father, please! I really want to play! I never get to compete!'

'Absolutely not Sarah. I can't believe you would even consider it.'

'Father, I just...'

'Sunday is for church and family. You should be thankful we let you go and watch the games at all.'

'Father, please! It's just women's netball!'

'You can go and watch like you usually do. But you may not play. And that's final.'

At the dinner table, Sarah pushed her potatoes around on her plate, quiet as her siblings chattered around her.

'Now, now, stop that, Sarah!' Phillip scolded. 'No sulking! I won't have that!'

Sarah quickly wiped her tears away, silencing her snivels. She had suddenly lost her appetite, but she forced her food down despite the growing lump in her throat.

On Sunday afternoon, Sarah sat in the grandstand and watched her teammates on the court, thoughts of disappointment and anger raced through her head. Her eyes watched the game, but her mind was preoccupied. She desperately wanted to compete in real competitions, but she was now certain that would never happen.

For a moment she entertained the thought of defying her father's orders and playing anyway. But Maleny was a small country town, and word would get back to her father.

The final whistle blew, and the spectators clapped and cheered. Sarah stood up and made her way down to the courts to congratulate her teammates on their victory, forcing a smile onto her face as she did every Sunday.

November brought blossoms to the Jacaranda trees all through the hinterland, the fallen purple flowers forming circular patches on the ground beneath. Crickets and geckos serenaded the balmy spring evenings. As the year drew to a close, Sarah sweltered in the classroom, pushing through the discomfort to complete her exams. She was determined not to let the heat affect her record of good grades, especially during her final year of school.

The bell clanged at three o'clock, and Sarah met Ron at the holding yard where they collected their horses.

'Gee, look at those storm clouds on the horizon,' she commented. 'They've come out of nowhere!'

'They're pretty dark,' Ron added. 'I hope we get home in time before it hits.'

Vivienne arrived shortly after with Bridget and Hilary, and after collecting her horse helped Hilary climb up into the saddle before mounting herself. Sarah doubled with Bridget, and Ron rode on his own. As they plodded along the road, they spotted wallabies popping their heads up above the grass and bouncing through the pastures.

Thunder rumbled in the distance, and Sarah felt the odd droplet of rain. The breeze quickened into wind, sweeping through the treetops and across the paddocks. It was a subtle warning that the thunderstorm was fast approaching.

'Come on, we need to get home,' Sarah hustled.

After securing their horses in the paddock, Ron, Sarah and Vivienne hurried to the house. Hilary and Bridget were already inside, and Aileen met them at the back door.

'Oh, thank goodness yer home in time!' she exclaimed.

The moment the last foot cleared the doormat the odd droplets multiplied, and within minutes unleashed into a heavy downpour. The tin roof amplified the sound. The wind threw gusts of water in a wild rhythm against the windows, as the landscape disappeared into the haze of the storm.

The rain eased as quickly as it had come. Aileen and the children opened the windows, and a cool breeze swept through the house. It was a refreshing change from the heavy humidity that had plagued them all day.

The afternoon storm brought in a cool evening, a relief from the humid, sticky nights spent kicking off sheets and tossing and turning in bed.

Aileen sliced the vegetables while Sarah stood at the stove, frying pieces of meat in a skillet.

'So, Sarah, I was talkin' with Mrs. Carlson at church, and young Patricia is off to secretarial college next year. It got me thinkin' that that would be something you should do next year. Secretarial work is a good job fer a woman, and ye could work in the church.'

'Actually, I would like to study nursing next year,' said Sarah.

'Nursing?'

'Yes. I've been talking with my friends, and the other girls at school. They're planning to do the same.'

Aileen shook her head and clicked her tongue. 'Nursing will not do, Sarah.'

'Why not?' asked Sarah, stunned.

'With secretarial work you can find a job in the church.'

'But I want to do missionary work, Mother. I can do that with nursing.'

'I won't see any of my daughters becomin' nurses, Sarah! Ye'll not be nursin' on my watch, ye hear? Those nurses get up te no good, smokin and drinkin. They'd be a bad influence on ye.'

Sarah turned back to the skillet. Aileen picked up her chopping board, turned to the stove and pushed the vegetables into a pot of boiling water.

'Come on, Sarah,' Aileen scolded, 'No misery. God won't be happy ter sees ye like that.'

Vivienne yawned and sat up in bed. Sarah was already awake, standing before her mirror and pinning her hair.

'Are you excited about today?' Vivienne asked.

'I don't know,' Sarah replied. 'It's hard to believe that this is my last day of school ever. This is it. I'll never go back.'

'It must feel strange,' Vivienne agreed.

'Girls, ye up,' Aileen hollered from down the hall.

'Yes, Mother!'

Rusty old trucks rattled along Maple Street churning up the dust, while ladies led their children between the stores as they ran errands and shopped for groceries. With her college application sealed in an envelope, Sarah approached the post office, stopping before the letterbox. With a heavy heart, she opened the lid and let the envelope slip through the slot, and out of her control. It was not the application she had wanted to send.

Chapter Four

At Christmas, Aileen brewed fresh ginger beer every year for the festive season, which kept the family refreshed during the hot summer days. She often packed a picnic for a trip to the creek at the bottom of the property, where the children spent hours swimming and canoeing. Sarah's grandmother came to stay with the family in Maleny over Christmas, and Sarah and Vivienne learned how to knit from her, while Sarah proudly demonstrated her playing skills on the piano.

In the New Year, while her younger sisters and brother returned to school, Sarah stayed at home awaiting word from the secretarial college in Brisbane. On Mondays she helped her mother hand wash the family's clothes. The baker visited at least once a week in his truck, his white apron caked with flour. The butcher came along as well. The family was self-sufficient in dairy and greengrocer products; they collected fresh eggs from the chickens, and every day Phillip brought home a pint of fresh milk, a portion of which Aileen churned into butter.

Phillip also maintained a thriving vegetable garden, and Aileen reared a healthy crop of watermelons that the family enjoyed between summer and autumn.

Once a week, Aileen made a trip into town to buy non-perishable items such as tea and flour, and also salt to add to the cream to make the butter. Before she left the house, she checked that she had the right amount of food stamps, proof that she was not getting more than her fair share. It had been five years since the war had ended, but the ghost of hardship still loomed over their small community.

On Sunday morning, Sarah caught a glimpse of her mother as she passed by her parent's bedroom, sitting at her dressing table in her nightdress. In their strict religious tradition, she had never cut her hair, and it reached all the way to her waist. She vigorously brushed handfuls of long brown locks and tossed it around, letting it tumble gracefully down her back. Aileen put the brush down and collected her hair into a ponytail, twisting it around and around itself on the top of her head. She fastened the bun into place with pins.

Each of the girls owned a pretty cotton summer dress to wear to church, along with one pair of gloves and dress shoes. Ron and Phillip fixed their neckties and pushed their felt hats onto their heads. The windows were left open, and the only reason the door was closed was to let potential visitors know they weren't at home. Phillip locked the front door and slipped the key under the front step. Bridget and Hilary sat in the dickey seat between their parents in the cabin of the Ford utility, while Sarah, Ron, and Vivienne settled down into the tray, holding onto the sides as they bumped along the dirt road toward town.

Maleny was deserted on Sundays. The church congregation were holding a special lunch after the service to farewell the young people leaving for Brisbane to attend college. Sarah laughed and chattered with her friends, and when it was time to leave, she said a bittersweet goodbye.

Sitting on her bed, Vivienne watched Sarah pack her young life into suitcases and hatboxes.

'So, tell me again, where are you going to live?' she enquired.

'With a family in Brisbane. The Franks. They're Brethren, and they live close to Shaw College.' Sarah sighed, placing a hand down on one of the hatboxes. 'I'm nervous, Viv. I've never been to the city. I guess it's all just sinking in now. It's real, but it's hard to believe.'

'I'll miss you Sarah,' said Vivienne. 'I can't talk to anyone like I can talk to you.'

Sarah sat down next to Vivienne and wrapped her arms around her. Vivienne leaned into her embrace, resting her head on Sarah's shoulder.

'I'll write to you every week. I promise,' Sarah insisted, wiping a tear trickling down her sister's cheek.

A gentle breeze swept through the grass in captivating visual waves as Sarah rode Dawn through the pastures. Thin clouds scattered across the blue sky, and the Blackall Ranges reached up out of the earth to meet them.

Sarah rode Dawn up the slope of the hill, stopping at the top and looking down over the farmland below. Old rusty windmills stood tall in the paddocks, the breeze slowly pushing their creaky blades around. The sun was falling in the sky and hit the horizon with golden brilliance. Sarah leant down and rested her head on the back of Dawn's neck, her tears trickling from her cheek onto Dawn's main. Their time together was coming to an end.

'I love you, Dawn,' she whispered. 'I always will. I will never, ever forget you. I will come and see you, I promise. Wherever I am, I will always have a part of you in my heart.'

The day of Sarah's departure arrived, and Aileen and the other children gathered in the front yard as Phillip loaded Sarah's luggage into the utility's tray.

Sarah and Vivienne held one another, crying quietly into each other's shoulders.

'Make sure you write to us every day, and tell us about everything,' Vivienne whimpered.

Sarah let go of Vivienne and embraced her other sisters, brother and mother.

'Ye'll be fine,' Aileen reassured with a shaky voice. 'The Franks sound like lovely people.'

Sarah climbed into the utility, leaning out the window and looked back at her family.

Once upon a time the days had come and gone, one after the other, simple and familiar. Sarah's life had consisted of school, church, house chores, sport, horse riding and spending time with her family. Her world had consisted of green pastures, cows, chickens and ducks. Her mother had always been there at the house to greet her when she arrived home from school. Now, for Sarah at least, the world had suddenly grown a little bigger.

Phillip drove into the township and followed the road out the other side. Sarah rested her arm on the window ledge, gazing out at the landscape, savouring the last moments in her beloved hometown. The land that she had grown up on seemed to scrape the sky. They spotted a drover on horseback up ahead and stopped to allow him to herd his sheep across the road from one paddock to the next. They wound their way down the mountain range along the curving country road; at one point, the edge of the road dropped off sharply into the valley below. Sarah could see down there tiny houses. To the south, she viewed the majestic Glass House Mountains, standing like giants above the land. In the far distance, she marvelled at the ocean, a blue giant that stretched all the way to the horizon.

The mountain road gradually evened out, and they arrived in Landsborough. The township was the gateway to the Blackall Ranges, and to the eastern coastal fishing village of Caloundra. They pulled up outside the train station, and Phillip unloaded Sarah's luggage, carrying it up to the small weatherboard Station Master's office. There, a man in a crisp white shirt, smart black vest and cap sat at the ticket window. Sarah grinned at his thick moustache, which reached down like handlebars past his mouth to his chin.

'Off to Brisbane?' he asked.

'Yes, please,' Phillip replied, slipping him a few shillings. 'One ticket, please.'

'There you go.'

Sarah blushed as the man nodded at her as he slipped a ticket back to Phillip.

The black steam train loomed large in front of Sarah as it stood at the station, hissing and puffing steam. The porter helped Phillip carry Sarah's bags to the luggage car. Two men stood up in the engine cabin, their overalls black with soot as they stocked the engine with coal. Sarah and Phillip joined a small group of passengers gathered on the platform.

'Mr. Frank will be waiting for you at Central Station,' Phillip stated. 'You take care of yourself, alright? You'll be fine.'

'Thank you, Father,' said Sarah quietly.

The engine driver sounded the whistle.

'All aboard!'

The passengers said their final farewells.

'You'd better hop on and get a seat,' said Phillip.

'Alright. Goodbye, Father.'

Sarah stepped up into the carriage picked a seat by the window. She jiggled the stiff, wooden window frame and pushed it upwards, hearing it click into place. She sat down, looking out at her father. He raised his hand, and her tears burned behind her eyes. She didn't want to go away. Not for secretarial college. She was thirteen years old and leaving the only home she'd ever known, to move to a faraway city and study a course in which she had absolutely no interest.

The whistle blew a second time, and the steel wheels of the train pushed forward in a slow, laborious rotation. Sarah looked out at her father for as long as she could. When she could no longer see him, she sat back in her seat, touching her handkerchief to her eyes, trying to conceal her sobs under her breath.

The train gathered speed as the wheels clickity-clacked along the tracks and the carriage rocked in rhythm side to side. Sarah gazed out at the endless bush land that flew past the window. The smoke from the engine smokestack blew into the carriage. She closed the window, took her book out of her satchel and settled into reading a novel she had chosen for the long trip.

The air in the carriage was hot and stifling. Sarah looked up, replaced the bookmark, and adjusted her glasses. She was surprised how the time had flown by, for now the train was approaching the outskirts of the city. There were more houses and less bush. As they entered the city area the houses were gradually being replaced by sandstone buildings.

They chugged along past suburban train stations, and Sarah noticed how many cars there were and how wide the roads were compared to her country township of Maleny.

There was an excited crowd waiting on the platform at Central Station. The chugging slowed into a long hiss as the breaks pulled the train to a heavy jolting stop. Sarah picked up her satchel and followed the other passengers to the rectangular wooden door at the end of the carriage. A man opened the door from the outside, and one by one the passengers carefully stepped down onto the platform.

'Sarah Ross?'

She turned to see a man approaching. He looked much like her father.

'Yes, that's me.'

'I'm Mr. Frank.'

'Oh, yes. It's lovely to meet you.'

'It's good to meet you. My car is parked just outside the station. It's not far to walk. Come on, let's fetch your bags.'

Mr. Frank was smartly dressed and clean-shaven. He looked much suaver than the rough farmers and tradesmen Sarah was used to seeing back at home. She followed him up a broad set of steps onto the main concourse. There were many people hurrying this way and that. Sarah had never experienced such a commotion. The architecture of the city buildings caught her attention. The arches of corrugated galvanized iron that formed shelters over the railway platforms, and a portico on Ann Street that ran alongside the station.

Outside, the city streets were bustling with cars and people. Mr. Frank stopped by one of the many cars parked outside the station and opened the passenger door.

'Thank you,' said Sarah as she sat on the buttoned leather seat of his spotless, clean car.

As Mr. Frank packed her luggage in the trunk, Sarah gazed up at the station. It was the biggest building she'd ever seen, so grand and elegant. A large clock tower stood tall above the main entrance.

As Mr. Frank drove through town, Sarah looked out at the tall buildings standing side by side along the streets.

'I could work in one of those buildings one day,' she thought to herself.

Brisbane had an excitement about it. Sarah felt exhilarated; she was sure there would be many opportunities for her once she had finished her secretarial course.

They passed a large rectangular building several stories high, with two wings adjoined in a V-shape. Several flags were raised and flapping about on the roof of the Brisbane General Hospital, and the medical school. It was there that Sarah wished that she would be going in just a few days, but it was not to be. A glimmer of hope flickered amidst her disappointment; she was young and had plenty of time to study nursing. If she just did what her mother wanted and then she could get on with her own plans.

The Franks lived on a tree-lined street with quaint houses, well-kept gardens and picket fences. As Mr. Frank unloaded Sarah's luggage, a woman came down the front steps to greet them. She wore a long brown dress buttoned all the way up to her neck. Her hair was fixed in a tight bun, the same way Aileen worn hers.

Mr. Frank took Sarah's suitcases and hatboxes inside, and Mrs. Frank showed her through the house. Sarah's spacious bedroom was a perfect square with a single bed positioned under the window. In the corner near the door stood a wardrobe, a study desk and a dressing table.

'I'm sure it's been an exhausting day for you,' said Mrs. Frank. 'I bet you could use a cup of tea.'

'Oh, yes please,' Sarah nodded, smiling. 'Thank you.'

Sarah sat with Mrs. Frank on the veranda, looking out over the garden. Mrs. Frank poured tea from the fine China pot into delicate china cup and saucers.

'It must be strange being away from home for the first time. Leaving your family.'

'Yes,' Sarah nodded. 'I've never been a long way from Maleny until today.'

'Well, this is your home as much as it is ours now, and I want you to feel comfortable. If there is ever anything you need, you be sure to ask me.'

Sarah spent the weekend settling in; on Sunday she attended church with the Franks, she received a warm welcome. She met some young people her age and they invited her to the youth group later in the afternoon.

On Monday morning, she caught the bus into town for her first day of college. Adjusting the strap of her satchel on her shoulder, Sarah hurried through the bustling halls of Shaw College. She was speechless at the very size of the school, the high ceilings and the long corridors. She felt so small and insignificant amongst all the girls and teachers. It was such a different atmosphere to primary school. Arriving at her classroom, she followed her fellow students inside and took a seat. Waiting for everyone to arrive was the teacher.

'Good morning, students,' she greeted. 'Please take your seats quickly.'

Sarah sat down at one of the wooden desks. She felt a mixture of excitement and nervousness. She had known everyone in her old school but here she knew no one. The class settled in, and the teacher stood before the blackboard.

Chapter Five

Dear Mother, Father, Vivienne, Ron, Hilary, and Bridget.

I'm sorry it's been a while since my last letter. I've been very busy at college these past few weeks, and I've been attending church with the Franks. I am also making lots of friends at college. I am really enjoying it here with them. I miss all of you very much and look forward to reading what you have been up to in your next letter.
Love, Sarah.

The weeks turned into months, and before too long Brisbane had become familiar. Maleny faded into the past, a memory of childhood. On her fourteenth birthday, Sarah received a card in the mail from her family, and Mrs. Frank cooked a special dinner. Yet despite the efforts of her host family, nothing could replace the presence of her real family, and Sarah felt their absence on her special day.

When her homesickness grew too much to bear, Sarah sat down to write another letter home, never mentioning how melancholy she felt in her weakest moments. She drowned out her sadness by immersing herself in her studies and social activities.

Christmas had seemed so far away, yet before Sarah knew it December arrived, and she was packing her bags to spend Christmas at home with her family. The year was over in the blink of an eye; looking back, the months had seemed like weeks, the weeks like days, and the days like seconds. Upon stepping off the train at Landsborough, Sarah spotted her father, running up to him and throwing her arms around him. He chuckled, staggering backward upon impact.

'Oh Father, I missed you so much!'

'We've missed you too, Sarah. Come on, let's get your bags.'

He paused before starting the car.

'Sarah, there's something I have to tell you,' Phillip confessed.

Sarah looked curiously at her father.

'What is it?'

Phillip sighed.

'Dawn passed away.'

'What?' Sarah managed to whisper though her shock, her voice breaking up through her tears. 'When?'

'It happened about a week ago. We wanted to wait until you were here to tell you. We didn't want you to be upset down in Brisbane all on your own.'

'Why did she die?'

'It was not long after you left that she fell ill. We tried to save her, but there was nothing we could do. She just got worse and worse as the time went on. I'm so sorry, Sarah.'

On the drive home Sarah gazed out the window hardly speaking a word. Finally, they drove through her humble hometown. The road that had taken her away was now taking her home.

Sarah stood heartbroken with Vivienne by the fence where Dawn had waited to meet her every day. Vivienne placed her hand on her shoulder.

'She missed you so much, Sarah.'

Sarah covered her mouth with her hand. Guilt, anger and sorrow flooded through her body. Her knees buckled underneath her, and Vivienne helped her to sit down on the grass.

'She died because of me,' Sarah sobbed. 'It was because of me!'

'No, no, Sarah,' Vivienne soothed, kneeling beside her.

'It was! It was my fault!'

'Sarah, this was not your fault, it's not our fault. Life is cruel sometimes. That's it.'

'Come on. Let's go back up to the house.'

'I just want to be alone for a while please Vivienne. Please.'

When Christmas was over, Sarah said goodbye to her family again and returned to Brisbane. The New Year commenced, and

Sarah returned to college. The days turned into weeks, the weeks to months.

Kneeling beside her bed, Sarah reached underneath and retrieved the shoe box in which she kept old letters from her family. Sitting up on the bed, she opened the delicate pieces of her mother's stationary, with the pictures of trees and birds in the corners of the pages, she breathed in deep the floral scent of the pretty writing paper.

Each letter consisted of short pieces of writing from each of her family, making up a collage of disjointed paragraphs. The handwriting dramatically changed as she scanned down the page, and she'd memorized which style belonged to which family member. She loved to trace her eyes around her mother's beautiful, cursive letters.

Much like Hilary and Bridget's, her father's writing was made up of untidy printed letters and spelling mistakes. Sarah knew he struggled with writing, but her mother always helped him. Ron wrote about working full-time with their father on the farm. Vivienne shared her challenges during her final year of school, and her plans to study dressmaking once she'd finished.

Sarah's second year in Brisbane ended, and the days grew warmer again.

'A letter has arrived for you Sarah.' 'What do they have to say this week?' Mrs. Frank asked as Sarah opened the letter.

Sarah's eyes lit up as she read down the page.

'They're moving to Brisbane!'

She looked up at Mrs. Frank, her smile stretching from ear to ear.

'My sister Vivienne finishes school at the end of this year, and she wants to go to college in Brisbane too! So, they're going to move the whole family down here!'

'Well, that's wonderful news!' Mrs. Frank exclaimed. 'You must be so eager to see them again.'

'Oh, I am! I can't believe this! I'm so excited! I miss them so much!'

Phillip and Aileen sold the farmhouse and bought a house in Chelmer, west of the Brisbane River. He would start work as a carpenter after they arrived in the new year.

The days grew longer and warmer, the Jacaranda and Poinciana trees exploded with purple and orange flowers. Sarah graduated from her secretarial course and spent Christmas with the Franks. Her family arrived in early January, and her father came to collect her.

'Thank you so much for having me,' she said graciously to her hosts.

'Oh, it was our pleasure,' said Mrs. Frank. 'It was so lovely having you stay with us. Please do keep in touch.'

Sarah chatted excitedly with her father as they drove to their new family home. They drove alongside the riverbank to Toowong, then across the Albert Bridge to Chelmer, to their new house on Leybourne Street. When the utility pulled up outside the house, Vivienne came running down the path, throwing her arms around Sarah. As they embraced, the aching hole of loneliness in Sarah's heart was finally filled. Vivienne stepped back, and Sarah grabbed at the ends of her sister's bobbed haircut.

'You cut off your braids!' she gasped.

'I know!' Vivienne giggled.

'You look so grown up!'

Aileen, Hilary, Bridget and Ron joined the reunion in the front yard.

'I'm so glad yer here,' Aileen beamed. 'Come inside!'

The modern house had a well-kept garden, and a fence surrounded the lawn. Next door was a small corner store, and they lived in walking distance to sprawling parks and the Brisbane River. Living in suburbia was so different to living on acreage in the old farmhouse.

Vivienne started training as a seamstress, while Hilary and Bridget started at the local school and Ron worked with his father learning to be a carpenter.

***

Standing on Adelaide Street, Sarah admired the stunning beauty of the Brisbane Arcade. It was so grand, with polished tiled floors, quaint glass shop fronts, and a high glass dome roof above.

'I wonder which store I will be working in,' Sarah wondered excitedly.

She looked down at the piece of paper with the shop's address. She looked up, tensed her brows, noticing a dark, narrow doorway tucked in between the arcade entrance and the glass shop front next door. She had missed it due to its insignificance. Beyond the doorway, she could see a wooden staircase, and her excitement deflated like a burst balloon.

'Do I have to go up there?' she asked herself.

She sighed heavily, stepping through the doorway. The stairs wound up and around, creaking under foot. There was a long corridor with musty old carpet. Sarah followed it down a short distance until she reached the Christian book shop door. Her mother had insisted she apply for this job.

She stepped inside, looking around. It was a small store, with shelves reaching the height and width of each wall which were full of books. The store was located in the middle of the building, and there were no windows. In the dim light, Sarah could see dust floating on the still, musty air. Tucked in the far corner was a solid wooden desk, and behind it sat a frail-looking old woman.

'Can I help you?' she asked.

'My name is Sarah Ross. I'm here for the job interview about the secretarial position?'

'Oh, yes. My name is Mrs. Hurst. Come and sit down.'

Mrs. Hurst wore a long black dress, her bony hands reaching

out of the frilly cuffs that trimmed her sleeves. She too wore her hair in the symbolic bun on top of her head. Sarah sat down opposite her at the desk and handed Mrs Hurst her college graduation certificate. Adjusting her glasses, Mrs. Hurst squinted in the poor light as she studied the page.

'Well, you don't have any experience, but you have the skills I require for the position. I have spoken with your mother about your character and religious beliefs.' The old woman looked over the top of her glasses at Sarah. 'You will be paid sixty shillings a week on Thursdays. You can start on Monday.'

***

It took Sarah two buses to travel from her family's house in Chelmer into the city. When she arrived at the bookstore, Mrs. Hurst took her past the front desk into a small back room.

'This is where you'll work.'

Boxes of books were stacked along the length of the walls and above their heads, shelves were stacked with paperwork and more books. A small desk was pushed into the corner, lit dimly by a lamp. In the middle of the desk sat a large, black typewriter.

'You'll do the accounts, place orders and keep track of them. The paperwork is all in alphabetical order. I have a system in place, and it must not be disorganized or changed.'

From Monday to Friday, Sarah started at nine o'clock and spent seven hours a day busily tapping away at the typewriter, straining her eyes in the dim light. At midday she spent her lunch break sitting in King George Square, breathing in the fresh air and sunshine. All the while, she waited longingly for the opportunity to become a nurse at the hospital only a short distance from the book shop.

28

Chapter Six

Sarah found a music school two blocks from the bookstore. Inside the building, a grand marble staircase led up to the first floor. She followed the hallway and stopped at one of the offices, knocking on the door. A middle-aged man answered; he wore a collared polo shirt, beige trousers and brown wingtip shoes. It was the fifties, and a lot of men in the city, especially the younger ones, wore this trendy new style of clothes. It was so different to the men Sarah had grown up with, whose attire was conservative for church and ragged and dirty for farm work.

'You must be Sarah.' The man spoke with poise and sophistication. 'It's lovely to meet you. I'm Mr. O'Neill. Please, come in and we'll get started.'

There were pictures hanging on the walls in the office, displaying photographs of people Sarah suspected were musicians. On the shelves were trophies of all shapes and sizes. The light from the sun streamed in through a large window, which was framed by royal red, velvet curtains. All those features complemented the elegance of the grand piano in the middle of the room. It commanded full attention. Sarah had never seen anything so beautiful.

'Please, take a seat,' Mr. O'Neill offered.

Sarah sat down at the piano, buzzing with excited anticipation as she rested her fingers gently on the keys.

'So, have you played much before?' Mr. O'Neill asked.

'I've been playing hymns since I was a little girl. I've never played a piano like this. Just the piano at home.'

'That's alright. That's why you're here - to learn.' He leaned back in his chair beside the piano. 'Play me your favourite hymn.'

Sarah hesitated.

'I don't bite,' Mr. O'Neill chuckled. 'Go ahead and show me what you can do.'

Although she was an amateur, Mr. O'Neill's nurturing presence brought her comfort. He focused on her hands as she played, nodding his head occasionally with the highs and lows of the notes.

'Wait,' Mr. O'Neill interrupted. 'Keep your wrists loose and high. If I may?'

Sarah shifted over on the bench seat and let him sit next to her. He began to play, his hands dancing up and down the keyboard. Sarah watched on in awe; his playing made it sound as if the piano were singing the song.

At the end of the lesson, Mr. O'Neill handed Sarah a music examination book.

'Here are some scales. This week, just practice the first line until you get it perfect. Next week we'll move onto the next line, alright?'

'Alright,' Sarah nodded, smiling. 'Thank you.'

Mr. O'Neill escorted Sarah to the door. 'I'll see you next Thursday afternoon.'

After her first lesson with Mr. O'Neill, Sarah's passion for music was ignited. The days spent stuck in the back office of the bookshop were serenaded by music playing over in her memory, making it all slightly more bearable. Now she had a new challenge of daily practice and weekly lessons to look forward to. It cost a large portion of her wage, but in Sarah's mind, it was money well spent.

Each week Mr. O'Neill gave Sarah a new section of music, and every evening she sat down at the old piano in her family's living room and practiced until she played the section flawlessly. Vivienne often watched and listened to her sister as she played.

Sarah finished the song, smiling and looking up at her.

'That's so beautiful, Sarah. You're so fluent!'

'Thank you. Mr. O'Neill thinks I will be ready to take my first exam soon.'

'Really?'

'Yes.'

'You'll do fine,' Vivienne assured. 'You always do well at anything you try. You always get good grades. Who knows, if we get an organ at church someday, you could play during the services!'

Sarah had only ever known the songs they sang in church, but now her eyes and ears had been opened to the world of classical music. She excelled at her first exam, and her confidence soared. She lost herself in her music; she loved how the piano had its own voice, and she could make it sound angry or sad, happy and bright or gentle and floating.

Happiness filled her heart every time she played. She enjoyed reciting her favourite hymns and singing along, hoping that someday they would indeed acquire an organ or piano at their church so that she could play during the Sunday services.

In the midst of her newfound confidence, the nursing dream that had been put to the back of her mind began to creep forward again, pulling at her heart and tempting her with the joy and fulfilment that awaited her in her dream career. She tried to push it all back into its deep, dark place, but it resisted, pushing forward. She was thinking about it more and more; during the lonely days at work, she found herself daydreaming about walking through hospital wards in her crisp white uniform. Her mother's stance on the subject was unlikely to have changed, but the daydreams persisted until she relented. She chose dinnertime to break the news.

'Mother, I had an interview at the hospital today.'

Aileen looked up at her daughter, frowning.

'An interview?'

'For nursing college. I picked up an application form too. I just need you to sign it.'

'What did I tell you about nursing, Sarah?'

'I know you don't like the idea,' Sarah continued, her voice quivering under her firm tone.

'I don't understand why ye girls don't want to work in the church. Ye sisters, they look up to ye, Sarah. Yer the eldest, remember? Ye show them the way. They do what ye will do.'

'And I would never encourage them to do anything wrong, Mother. But it's what I want to do. I want very much to study nursing, Mother. I feel it will contribute to my missionary work someday. Just like I told you.'

Aileen huffed, shaking her head as she continued to cut up the vegetables.

Standing a few feet from the letterbox on the street corner, in her hands Sarah held a plain white envelope. People hurried all around her, and cars roared by in both directions.

'Is this right', she thought.

Her legs felt like concrete as she stepped forward. Her heart pounding in her chest, she reached up to the slot, but quickly pulled her hand back.

'What if I was wrong? Should I really be doing this?'

The letterbox was just an ordinary object, an everyday utility on the corner of a busy city street, yet it was the gateway to her dreams. Her heart was torn between loyalty and ambition, between her mother's wishes and her own heartfelt desires. She had never disobeyed either of her parents in her entire life, and the prospect of doing so brought a sense of crushing guilt.

Sarah reached forward again and opened the lid, and with a deep breath released her fingers and let the letter slip inside. In that moment, she felt the eyes of her mother upon her. She knew that if her application was accepted, the dynamics of her family life would change forever.

She turned and walked back up the street toward the bookstore, finding the crushing guilt fleeting in a moment, replaced by a new excitement rushing through her body. Her steps became bolder, and she pulled her shoulders back and held her head high. She could taste her dream; she felt strong and wanted to dance and scream with exhilaration.

Lying on her bed reading a book, Sarah looked up and saw Vivienne come into the bedroom. She sat up, watching Vivienne sink down onto her bed, visibly shell-shocked from the confrontation with their mother.

'How did it go?' Sarah enquired.

Vivienne shrugged.

'We talked it over, and she seems okay, I guess.' She exhaled heavily. 'She just doesn't understand. I want to be a nurse too, not a dressmaker! We'll be helping people! How could that be wrong?'

Sarah nodded.

'Mother will come around. Just give her time.'

Part Two
The Rose Blossom

Chapter Seven

The hum of chatter could be heard amongst the guests as they found their seats in the college hall. Students from hospitals far and wide, from Brisbane to the Gold and Sunshine Coasts, had gathered there for their graduation ceremony.

The evening opened with two solo vocal performances, and Sarah gave a solo piano performance. The Chairman of the University Board welcomed the Minister for Health and Home Affairs, who proceeded to call upon the students to receive their general nursing certificates.

When it was Vivienne's turn, Sarah clapped and cheered as her sister stepped forward, leading the applause that lifted from the audience. Vivienne shook the Minister's hand, and a photographer took their picture as she received her certificate.

Following the presentation, the Matron of the Hospital led the students in reciting the Florence Nightingale Pledge for Nurses.

Sarah and Vivienne began work at the Brisbane General Hospital, whilst returning to college almost immediately to become Nursing Sisters. At the start of each week, Sarah and Vivienne packed clothes and toiletries into their travel bags, and together they caught two buses across town to the hospital. They had quickly come to dislike their extensive weekly commute.

From Monday to Thursday, they attended lectures at the medical school in the morning and began a shift of work at the hospital in the afternoon or evening. They learned on the job, under the instruction of the Head Nurse of the ward to which they were assigned. They slept in two-bed dormitories, and on Friday evenings caught the bus home and spent the weekend with their family.

Sarah passed her previous exams with high distinctions, and two years later she and Vivienne graduated again. Sarah was placed in charge of a ward, and from day to day she supervised the nurses in her charge and allocated their duties. She accompanied doctors on their rounds, alerting them to any concerns or complaints regarding the patients. She befriended the patients in her ward and became a welcome face to them during their stay. She was living her dream.

Every Christmas the Ross family attended youth camp at Burleigh Heads on the Gold Coast. There were many other teenagers and young adults, from both local and Brisbane-based church youth groups. Sarah wound down the car window, resting her chin on top of her folded arm, smiling as she breathed in the fresh air, feeling the salty breeze against her face. Driving along the Esplanade, they passed single storey restaurants, shops and accommodation flats. A green, grassy picnic area backed onto the beach, divided from the sand by a stretch of Norfolk Pine trees.

They spent the morning at the beach, and then drove to the campsite nearby. They pulled into the driveway, where several other cars were already parked.

Behind them was the high-set, one-level weatherboard mess hall, where all the meals were served, camp activities and church services were held. A single row of timber cabins was situated on either side of the building; one side was for the males and the other for the females. Sarah, Vivienne, Ron, Bridget, and Hilary were all hut leaders and were required to arrive a day earlier than the rest of the campers. Phillip and Aileen stayed on and helped out in the kitchen.

That evening, the leaders and camp parents, Clayton and Dot Brooker, remained in the mess hall after dinner to discuss the week's activities. Afterwards, they all enjoyed a light supper. Talking with her friends, Sarah felt a tap on the shoulder. She turned to see Clayton and Dot's son, Jack, standing before her. He smiled a crooked smile because of his hair lip. Jack was a lovely young man; although extremely shy, he always made the effort to say hello.

'Jack,' she greeted. 'Hi!'

'How are you, Sarah?'

'Good, thanks. It's great to see you again!'

'You, too,' Jack agreed. 'So, what have you been up to?'

'Oh, I've been really busy at the hospital. I'm a Head Sister now.'

'Wow! Congratulations!'

'So, what have you been doing,' Sarah enquired.

'Oh, still painting houses with my father.'

The following morning, the cars and buses of campers arrived. In the evening they gathered in the mess hall for dinner. There were two single rows of the bench tables separated by an aisle down the middle. Sarah sat with the girls from her hut, waiting to be instructed to join the line to collect their dinner. Her eyes wandered to one of the boy's tables, where she noticed a new hut leader. She had seen him at the meeting the previous night. She thought he had such a lovely smile, and friendly eyes. He was fit and tanned, like most young men his age from working out in the sun. He spotted her and she quickly looked away, hoping he didn't think she had been staring at him.

The sun was shining, and the days were warm. Campers packed their beach bags with towels and snacks and gathered in the driveway.

Sarah walked with her friend Janelle and a few other leaders, chatting and giggling with the girls in their charge. They followed the Esplanade along, crossed the grassy park and the Norfolk pines to re-grouped on the beach. As the other campers rushed past them to the water, Sarah and her friends laid their towels out on the sand.

'Oh, this weather is just glorious!' Janelle exclaimed.

The girls conversed about their jobs and what they had been up to since the last camp. Sarah reached into her bag and took out a Box Brownie.

'Sarah! You've got your own camera!' Janelle gasped.

'Yes, I bought it myself. Now, everyone gather together for a picture!'

The girls shuffled together on the towels and Sarah held the camera in front of her chest. She looked down into the viewer, which reflected the image that would be taken. She pressed down the button on the front and took the picture, and then wound the film on with a small handle on the side.

Just as Sarah was putting the camera back in its case, she was startled when a hard object hit her in the back of the head.

'Ouch!' she cried, looking to see a beach ball lying behind her.

'George! Be careful!'

'Sorry, Jan,' said the young man as he bent down to pick up the ball.

'Don't apologize to me, say it to Sarah!'

Sarah looked up to see the face she'd been gazing at in the mess hall.

'I'm sorry,' he repeated.

Janelle sighed, rolling her eyes.

'Sarah, this is my cousin. George, this is my friend, Sarah.'

'Nice to meet you, Sarah,' George smiled. 'May I sit down?'

'Sure,' Sarah shyly agreed.

The other girls cooed mockingly, and Janelle smirked.

'I meant to say hello at the leaders meeting last night,' George continued. 'So, how long have you been coming to this camp?'

'Oh, since I was a child.' Sarah tucked a wave of hair behind her ear. 'My Father and Grandfather helped built it.

'What about you?'

'My family just moved up from New South Wales. This is my first year of camp. So, what do you do when you're not here?'

'I'm a Ward Sister at Brisbane General Hospital.'

'Wow,' George exclaimed. 'I'm impressed!'

'Thanks.' Sarah nodded. 'I love it. I want to work as a

missionary someday.'

Lunchtime approached, and the leaders called the kids in their charge to start their walk back to camp. Sarah and George picked up their towels, and once they had gathered their groups together, they began walking up the beach toward the park.

The afternoon air was cool, and Sarah wrapped her towel tightly around her body. Her hand slipped and she felt her fingers brush George's. She held her breath a moment; he must have felt it too. Her heart fluttering, she looked the other way.

'Sarah, is that your boyfriend?' sang her group of girls.

Sarah looked away from George, with a coy laugh, her cheeks blushing red. George might have been embarrassed too, but she couldn't bring herself to look at him to see.

Every day of camp was packed with activities. During the day, campers went for bushwalks and swam at the beach, and at night played games in the mess hall. Sarah and George spent as much time as they could together in and around their duties as hut leaders.

The week ended, and it was time to return home. Sarah heaved her suitcase into the trunk of her family's car. Her heart danced at the very thought of George and was also heavy with the reluctance to say goodbye.

'Sarah?'

She turned from the car to see him standing before her. In his hand he held a piece of paper and a pencil.

'Can I have your phone number please?'

'Sure.' Sarah said trying hard to contain her excitement as she wrote her number.

On the drive home, her family's chatter about the week at camp, faded into the background as Sarah daydreamed about her past week. Gazing out the window at the sun sparkling on the calm, flat water, she wished there could be one last swim before the return to regular life, one last day spent in paradise. She wondered how after only one week George could suddenly command such a longing in her heart.

Chapter Eight

Standing tall before her bedroom mirror, Sarah pinned the small cap over the crown of her head. Brushing her hands over her crisp white uniform blouse and skirt, she regarded her reflection with proud satisfaction. Beneath her uniform, her tender, sun kissed skin was a painful souvenir from her week at the beach. As she made her rounds at the hospital, the thought of George was never far from her mind.

Each time the home telephone trilled, Sarah came bounding into the living room in anticipation, and finally one evening, the call was indeed for her. Twirling her fingers around the curly phone cord, the sounds of her family disappeared as she listened with ease to the sound of George's voice. When he asked her for a date, she accepted his invitation without hesitance. He would pick her up from her house and meet her parents as well.

The night of the date arrived, and Aileen answered the door.

'Ye must be George,' Aileen beamed at the handsome, smartly dressed young man on her doorstep.

'Yes. Mrs. Ross, nice to meet you.'

'Come on in. Sarah won't be long.'

Folding his newspaper, Phillip stood and shook George's hand.

'It's good to meet you properly, George.'

'And you too sir,' George nodded.

'Can I get ye a glass of water, George?' Aileen inquired.

'Yes please, Mrs. Ross.'

'Sit down,' Phillip invited. 'So, George, I understand you met Sarah at camp?'

'Yes, that's right.'

'Which church are you from?'

'George?'

The two men turned and stood to meet Sarah as she entered

the living room.

'Sarah, you look lovely!' George exclaimed.

'Thank-you,' Sarah blushed.

'So, where are you both off to tonight?' Phillip asked.

'To a social night at my youth group,' George said.

'We won't be late,' Sarah added.

Walking to the car, Sarah smiled coyly, her eyes fixed on the footpath. George reached over and pried one of her hands clutching her purse. She held her breath. He smiled as he held her hand for the first time.

George had a mysterious twinkle in his eye, as if he could see right through Sarah's efforts to contain her awkward nervousness. There seemed to be no fooling him.

They had an exciting evening as they announced to their friends that they were 'boyfriend and girlfriend'. At the end of the evening, George pulled up outside Sarah's house and turned the car off. He turned to face her; his eyes were kind, gentle and welcoming. Although she couldn't bring herself to look right into them, she couldn't resist them.

'Did you have a nice time?' he asked.

'Yes, I did, thank-you,' Sarah nodded.

He paused, smiling.

'Sarah,' he chuckled. 'I don't really know how to say this.'

Sarah looked up at him; for the first time since they'd met, she watched his sleek and confident persona melt away, exposing a sheepish vulnerability.

'I've never felt this way about anybody before. You're so different.'

He paused, and the silence was filled with the sound of Sarah's heart pounded in her ears.

'I guess what I'm trying to say is, I think I'm falling for you. I think I'm in love with you…I've been trying to figure out how to say it to you. It is so soon, and I was a little scared of how you might react.'

'It's okay,' Sarah whispered, her voice trembling.

George reached over and stroked her hair.

'You're so beautiful.'

He leaned across and pressed his lips softly against hers. There was no noise, no thoughts, and no world. Moments later George gently pulled his lips away, and the two looked at one another, equally lost for words.

'I had better go inside,' Sarah stammered.

'I'll walk you in,' George insisted.

George opened the car door for Grace, and the two walked hand in hand to the front door, standing on the step.

'Goodnight, George.'

Sarah stepped inside, walking slowly down the hallway, startled by her parents sitting in the living room. Aileen looked up from her book.

'Hello dear. How was yer night?'

'It was fine.'

Aileen paused a few moments.

'Are ye right?'

'Yes, yes, I'm fine.'

Aileen nodded.

'Alright then. See ye in the mornin'.'

'Goodnight,' Sarah agreed, slipping into her bedroom.

She quietly closed her bedroom door, tiptoeing to her bed. She collapsed onto her front, burying her face in her pillow and squealing.

'Sarah?' She looked around, seeing Vivienne sit up.

'How did it go?'

'Vivienne, I love him!' she exclaimed, rolling onto her back and throwing her arms up over her head.

She glanced cautiously at the door, clasping her hand over her mouth and giggling. Vivienne scampered across the room to

Sarah's bed.

'It was so wonderful. It was as if I were in a dream!' She placed her hand over Vivienne's. 'He told me he loved me!'

'He did?'

Vivienne's eyes were wide as she slapped her hand over her own mouth.

'Yes. He did. I've never felt this way before.'

'Oh, Sarah, I'm so happy for you!' Vivienne shrieked.

'Shhh' Sarah hissed, and she and Vivienne giggled softly.

'I can't believe it,' she continued. 'I'm so in love! I can't understand it; it's all just racing through me! I'm excited and terrified all at once! I just want to shout, and tell the world, 'I love him!' a million times over and over again!'

What she felt for George felt free and beautiful, gushing uncontrollably from her heart. Navigating her feelings for George, Sarah felt as if she was stumbling through unfamiliar territory. Every moment spent away from him was unbearable, and every moment she spent with him was never enough. She felt as if she was going mad; George had completely unravelled her, consuming her thoughts every moment of the day. She had never experienced such extreme emotional contrasts of love and longing before in her life, pulling her heart in such opposite directions. What was wrong with her, she wondered.

As the weeks passed, Sarah felt her nervousness melting away, letting her guard down to allow her own strong personality show through. She challenged George with her wit and knowledge, and over the course of the next month she and George learned more about one another, discovering a shared love for life and for their religious faith.

Chapter Nine

The single rose rested in a vase on Sarah's dressing table. George had given it to her on their last date. The blossom was in full bloom, an adequate reflection of her life. She had her dream career and a boyfriend she adored. The plan for her life was on track, and everything was perfect.

After dinner one night Sarah and Vivienne huddled in bed together under the covers.

'Sarah, what does it feel like to fall in love?' asked Vivienne.

Sarah sighed, gazing up at the ceiling.

'When he leaves, you want to be with him still. You can barely think until the next time you see him, and you feel like you're going to go crazy until you do.'

She paused, looking at Vivienne.

'I've never felt anything like it before.'

Sarah nuzzled her head onto her sister's shoulder.

'I've never 'loved' anyone before, but since the first time I saw him, I knew I loved him. I knew straight away that I could marry him. I know I could be with him for the rest of my life. Not just because Mum and Dad say I should marry him, but also because I want to. And I love that. I've never really thought about what I wanted in a husband, but somehow I just know George is all I need.'

'Can I be your Maid of Honour when you two get married?'

'Yes, of course you can!'

'I can't wait to fall in love. I hope I can feel as happy with someone one day as you do with George.'

'You will, Vivi. You will.'

***

Sarah and George shared a brief kiss at the door before Aileen came down the hallway and greeted George with open arms. They sat together at the table with the family; everyone was present except for Vivienne, who was working the night shift at the hospital. Aileen served corned silverside and vegetables. The cutlery clattered around the table as everyone started to eat.

'So, George, ye and Sarah have been spendin' a lot of time together,' Aileen enquired. 'Ye must be very fond of each other.'

George smiled at Sarah.

'Yes, Mrs. Ross. I care about Sarah very much.'

'I saw that lovely rose ye gave 'er. It is very beautiful indeed. Yer seem like a good man, George. It is a pleasure to have ye in our home.'

'Thank you, Mrs. Ross. It is a pleasure to be here with all of you.'

As her family conversed with George, Sarah observed the picture playing out before her. It was perfect: George and her father got along so well, and everybody loved him.

'So, George, which church do you go to?' Phillip enquired.

'The Baptist church in Indooroopilly.'

Silence fell upon the table. Sarah looked to her father, and then her mother.

'George has been a camp leader down in New South Wales since he was a teenager,' she chimed in. 'Just like us.'

Aileen coldly nodded.

'I see.'

George looked curiously at Sarah, and she smiled nervously, poking her vegetables with her fork. The once flowing conversation had become stifled and stagnant. After dinner Aileen made tea, and at the end of the evening, Sarah walked George to his car.

'Was everything alright tonight?' he asked. 'The mood seemed to turn a bit after I told your parents I was Baptist.'

'Oh, never mind,' Sarah dismissed, trying to make light of the awkward situation. 'My parents are just getting to know you, that's all. Just adapting to the fact you're not 'Brethren', probably. That you're not 'one of us'.'

'I see,' George said.

Sarah touched his arm.

'Please, don't worry. I know they're fond of you.'

She waved to George as he drove down the street. She turned back to the house, taking a deep breath as she walked up to the door. She found her mother in the kitchen drying dishes. Aileen narrowed her eyes at Sarah, her thin lips pressed firmly together. Sarah looked around.

'Where is everybody?'

'I asked them ter go ter their rooms. Yer father and I need ter speak with ye alone.'

'What's wrong?'

'Sit down, please.'

Sarah took a seat with her parents at the table.

'What happened at dinner earlier? Why did you all go so quiet?'

'He's a Baptist?'

Sarah shrugged. 'So.'

Aileen shook her head. 'Their belief is different to ours!'

Sarah rolled her eyes.

'Just because he's not from our church doesn't mean he's not a good Christian, Mother. He loves God just as much as we do! I assure you!'

Aileen insisted. 'You must marry a Brethren man.'

'Mother, I don't doubt the strength of his faith for a moment! I am so thankful that he has been brought into my life!'

Sarah paused. The atmosphere was thick with tension.

'Mother, George is a good Christian man.'

Aileen shook her head profusely. Sarah looked at her father.

'Father, you've talked with George, you've got to know him! He's a good man, isn't he? Please, tell her!'

Phillip's eyes dropped to the table.

'Come on, Father! Please, I know you agree with me!'

'I'm sorry, Sarah,' he said quietly, looking up at her. 'I can't condone this. This is not our way.'

Sarah felt the tears burning behind her eyes.

'What are you talking about? What are you saying?'

'You're not to see that boy anymore, Sarah,' Aileen continued. 'I forbid it.'

Sarah stood and ran down the hallway, throwing herself onto her bed and sobbing into her pillow. Her heart felt as if it had been stabbed with a knife, and life was bleeding out of her.

'I won't let you go! I don't care what anyone says! I won't let you go!'

Chapter Ten

After a long time strumming her fingers against the wall, Sarah lifted the telephone receiver from the cradle and dragged her fingers around the number dial. She waited, glancing at her mother and sisters in the kitchen, her father in the living room reading the paper.

'Hi George, its Sarah. Can you come over?'

Sitting by the window in the living room, Sarah gazed blankly out into the yard. George's car pulled up outside. She pushed herself out of the chair, and George's smile faded a little as she came down the path. He placed his hand on her shoulder.

'Sarah, is everything alright?'

'George, can we take a walk?'

Strolling along the footpath toward the park in Leybourne Street, George turned and looked at Sarah.

'Please tell me what's wrong,' he urged.

She looked up at him.

'George, I can't see you anymore.'

'Wait, what?'

George stopped the two of them, looking at her in alarm.

'It's hard to explain,' Sarah hesitated.

'I think I deserve to know,' George probed.

'George, please,' Sarah begged.

'What is it, Sarah? What happened?'

Sarah looked down at the pavement; again, she found that she could not look him in the eye. At the end of a long sigh, she spoke again.

'I can't see you anymore because you're a Baptist.'

'What?'

'My family is Brethren. They don't believe that your faith is as 'true' as ours.'

'That's ridiculous!' George scoffed. 'Sarah, that's absurd!'

'George, I'm on your side. This is hard for me. I'm the one that has to face my family!'

'They will get used to it! They got used to you being a nurse!'

'They won't forgive me for this, George.'

George went to speak, and then stopped himself. Sarah took the opportunity.

'George, if I keep going with you my family will disown me. They will. My church will shun me. We will never have a normal life together; it will always be difficult.'

She paused.

'They are my family, George. I love them. They're all I've ever known. And I'm scared of losing them...' Her voice trailed off, and she looked away again. 'I'm scared.'

George took her hands in his and held them against his chest as he looked intently into her troubled tear-filled eyes.

'Sarah, do you think Vivienne would ever disown you? I don't think so. You will never lose her, Sarah. I've seen the two of you together. Nothing would ever tear you apart.'

He gently squeezed her hands. Sarah closed her eyes, and George lifted her chin with his finger to make her look at him again.

'You're smart, kind, you're a good Christian woman! I want to be with you! And I know you want to be with me, you're just scared! It will be alright in time, trust me!'

'George, I...'

'Does it really matter to you what church I go to?' He reached up and gently wiped a tear away from her eye with his thumb.

George knelt before her.

'Sarah, will you marry me?'

She laughed once, throwing her head back.

'Would you be my wife?' George persisted. 'Will you let me look after you? I'll start coming to your church...'

Sarah pinched her mouth to one corner. George kissed her

hands.

'I'm sorry, George. It's not that simple.'

He looked up at her, his smile fading.

'I wish I could, but I couldn't live with myself. The rejection of my family would be too much for me.'

She withdrew her hand from his.

'I'm so sorry,' she whimpered. 'I have to go.'

She turned and hurried back toward the house, ignoring his desperate calls. She reached the gate, hurrying up the front path, and briefly caught her mother's gaze as she passed the living room. In her bedroom, she sat down on the edge of her bed, panting over her racing heart. She removed her glasses, lowered her head, and cried.

For hours she cried loud and painful. Just as the love had spilled out of her heart, so now did the agony. As the light faded, she lay in the middle of her bed, exhausted and numb, her face soaked wet with her tears.

'What have I done?' she whimpered.

Chapter Eleven

As it had been since they met, the first thought that popped into her head when she woke was of George, but this morning the thought brought sadness rather than joy. She wanted to wake up one morning with no memory of him, or of the love they'd shared. The sight of him kneeling on the pavement as she turned and walked away haunted her every moment of the day. She would never again feel his loving arms around her, nor be warmed by his smile. The despair was unbearable, but life pressed on and didn't wait for her to re-gather the pieces of her broken heart. She forced herself to face the day with the gaping hole in her heart where George had been ripped out. She had no choice but to move on and find a suitable husband in order to shut her mother up. She knew that it was the only way she would ever live in peace.

At Easter time the Ross family returned to the Gold Coast for the youth camp. As they drove, the scenery that had once brought Sarah excitement now only re-ignited the painful memories.

When they arrived at the campsite, she forced a smile onto her face and did her best to act happy as she greeted her friends. They seemed to have forgotten her recent ordeal and presumed she had moved on by now. Surrounded by familiar faces, she looked nervously out of the corner of her eye, but she didn't see him anywhere. She sighed and shook her head. She felt paranoid about bumping into George.

The leaders gathered in the mess hall that night, catching up on each other's activities in the months since Christmas. She was relieved that there was no sight of George. She saw that Jack was there. Determined to move on, she crossed the room and tapped him on the shoulder.

'Hi, Jack. How are you?'

'Good thanks. It's great to see you again. How's the year been for you so far?'

'Oh, very busy. Very busy. You know, work, church, all those things.'

'Can I make you a cup of tea?' Jack offered.

'Oh, yes please,' Sarah agreed.

'So where did you go to school, Jack?' Sarah enquired as she walked with him, the other leaders and the campers to the beach.

'In The Grange, the suburb where my family live. But when I was eight I was sent to a special school.'

'Why?' Sarah gasped.

'My hair lip. The teachers thought I was stupid because of the way I talked, but it's just my lip. It's not my brain.' Jack sighed. 'Anyway, I left that school when I was thirteen, and started working with my father in our family's house painting business.'

Sarah sighed. 'You don't sound strange when you speak.'

'I've taught myself to talk normal, like everybody else.' Jack pulled a funny face.

'I'm sorry to hear you had to go through that, Jack. I really am. It sounds like life has been hard for you.'

Jack shrugged.

'I've learned a lot of skills, although my father is really tough to work with.' He chuckled. 'He has been on my back about getting married. But between work, cycling and church activities, I've just been so busy these past few years.'

'You're not alone there either,' Sarah laughed. 'My mother calls me an old maid and a spinster. It's really hurtful.' She paused. 'So, you mentioned cycling?'

'Yes, bicycle racing,' Jack replied. 'I train a few times a week with a team.'

'Oh, really? Do you ever compete?'

'Well, no. The competitions are always held on Sundays, and my father won't hear of it.'

'Ha, you too.'

The week came to an end, and once back in Brisbane Jack took Sarah on a date. They saw each other a few times a week, and Jack spent time with Sarah's family.

Sitting in their dormitory room at the hospital between their shifts, Sarah and Vivienne nibbled away at a box of chocolates Jack had given Sarah.

'So how do you feel about Jack?' Vivienne asked, scanning the box for her next selection.

'I'm happy,' Sarah sighed. 'He is a good man, and well respected in the church. He is so funny; he makes me laugh. He has such a dry sense of humour.'

***

After an evening date, Jack opened the car door for Sarah and took her hand to help her out of the car.

'Sarah, I have something to give you. I've been waiting for the right time.'

Reaching into his pocket he knelt before her, and Sarah held her breath as he opened the small box.

'Will you marry me?'

'Oh, my goodness!' Sarah gasped.

Jack smiled.

'I must ask your father before I give you the ring, but I'm sure it will all be fine. I'll speak to him tomorrow.'

Sarah looked down at the ring, delicately touching the band.

'It is lovely, Jack. It really is. I'm…I'm speechless.'

Inside, Vivienne was sound asleep in her bed. Sarah stretched out on her bed and gazed up at the shadowy shapes dancing on the ceiling as the moonlight streamed in through the sheer curtains. She had been expecting the proposal; her mother had been playfully persistent about her expectations and was not ashamed to voice them when Jack came for dinner.

Yet still it had taken Sarah by surprise. She thought back to that afternoon in late January, when George had knelt before her on the pavement, and asked her the same question. Amidst the flurry of excitement, the dreaded pang of regret jabbed at her heart, but she pushed it back, pushed it down, back down into the depths out of sight and out of mind.

Chapter Twelve

Sarah had seen many different reflections of herself in the mirror over the years: a school student, a nurse, and then a Ward Sister. And now, she was a bride.

Her hair was set under her veil. On her hands she wore lace gloves, and her gown reached all the way to the floor. It was the most beautiful dress which Vivienne had made for her. Together with her sparkling engagement ring, she felt like a princess.

Her sisters entered the bedroom, wearing the baby blue bridesmaid dresses that Vivienne and Bridget had also made for them.

'Oh, Sarah, you look absolutely amazing!' Vivienne exclaimed. 'How do you feel?'

'I don't know,' Sarah chuckled. 'I'm really nervous.'

'You'll be fine! You're so beautiful! Jack is going to be speechless when he sees you!'

Standing at the church doors, Sarah slipped her hand into the crook of her father's arm. The lady on the organ played, and they began their walk down the aisle, the guests beamed at Sarah from the pews. Standing with his groomsmen at the altar, Jack smiled proudly as Sarah came towards him.

'Who gives this bride to be married.' The minister solemnly asked.

'I do.' Philip placed Sarah's hand in Jack's, and they turned to face the minister.

With confetti floating in the air, the guests cheered as Jack and Sarah exited the church and climbed into Jack's A40 Austin utility. Sarah waved back at her wedding guests as they drove out of the carpark, towing a small 1940s model caravan behind them. They headed north to Bundaberg, a six-hour drive from Brisbane, where they spent the week visiting friends and relatives and enjoying much needed time off work. For the first time, Sarah experienced her new husband outside the world of their church and families.

Her love for Jack was different to that which she had felt for George. It was less romantic, less heart pounding. Jack was gentle and sweet to her, and Sarah felt peaceful and comfortable in his presence. Their past hardships had brought them together; their difficult relationships with their parents were something they had in common. Sarah felt a connection with Jack due to their similar strict religious family lives. Now they had their parents' and church community's support in their marriage.

Jack had warmed her heart with friendship, and the pain of losing her previous relationship had eased. The hole of loneliness in her heart had been filled, just as she'd intended by developing the relationship with Jack. And now that she was married, her mother was satisfied. At last, she was free to get on with her career.

At the end of the week the Austin A40 pulled up in front of the highset Queenslander style house in The Grange, a northern suburb of Brisbane. Jack's mother Dot came down the front steps to greet them.

'Welcome home!' she called. 'Did you have a nice time?'

'Yes, thank you,' Sarah replied.

Clayton helped Jack carry the suitcases inside to the back bedroom, where Sarah and Jack would stay for the next few months until their own house was built.

'I still don't know why you would want to live in Keperra,' Clayton scoffed over dinner that night. 'It's at the ends of the earth! All that's out there is acreage properties!'

'The land was affordable,' Jack insisted.

'The Housing Commission style of home is very popular at the moment,' Sarah added. 'We will have a view over the back paddock and the crop farm from the kitchen window…'

'How much did you pay for it?'

'Three hundred pounds,' said Jack. 'I've got the approval for the loan from the bank for two thousand dollars to finish building.'

'Oh, that's good news dear Jack.' Aileen said.

'What is Sarah going to do sitting out there on her own all day while you're at work?'

'Oh, I'll be at work most days in the city, Mr. Brooker,' Sarah chimed in.

'But what about when you have children?'

'Well, I'm sure we'll work it out when that happens,' Jack interrupted. 'It will be a good place to raise a family.'

Sarah sat on the small front veranda, sipping tea from her cup. The door opened and Jack stepped outside.

'This is only temporary, sweetie,' he assured. 'We'll be in our own house soon enough.'

'Oh, I know,' Sarah nodded, smiling. 'It's fine.'

Jack rose at five o'clock in the morning, moving around making noise as he dressed for work. He left the bedroom, and Sarah could hear him and Clayton talking in the kitchen. The little radio on the table blared the morning news. A few minutes later Jack returned, carrying a cup of tea on a saucer.

'Oh, thank you, darling,' Sarah said graciously as he set it down on the bedside table.

'You're welcome.' Jack leaned down and gently kissed her forehead. 'Have a good day.'

'You too, dear.' said Sarah.

He turned and left the room, closing the door behind him. Later in the morning, Sarah dressed in her uniform. She was glad to be going back to work at the hospital.

Three months after the wedding the house was finally finished. Sarah stood out on the back steps, admiring the surrounding acreage properties. On one side was a house belonging to another young married couple. The other side was a stretch of native bushland, with the owner's house perched up on the distant hill. At the back fence of all the properties was farmland. It was like living in the country, and it took Sarah back to Maleny.

Keperra was indeed a long way out of town and even further from her family, but that was how Sarah liked it. Here, she could live the way she wanted, away from her mother's constant dictations.

Possums jumped from branch to branch in the gum trees as the evening fell upon them. Jack stood behind Sarah on the steps, wrapping his arms around her. 'Finally, here we are,' he sighed.

Sarah rested her head back against his chest.

'I know. It's all ours. It's so quiet and peaceful. I love it.'

'I'm glad,' Jack said.

Sarah smiled contently, stroking his hand. She turned her head, tenderly kissing her husband.

Sarah and Vivienne sat together at one of the tables in the hospital cafeteria. Placing her cup of tea down in the saucer, Vivienne paused thoughtfully, looking at her sister.

'Sarah, I have something to tell you.'

'What is it?' asked Sarah.

'Larry proposed!'

'Oh, Vivi!' Sarah gasped. 'But isn't he a Baptist?'

'Yes, he is.'

'Have you told Mother?'

'Not yet.' Vivienne sighed. 'But you know what, I don't care what Mother and Father say! I don't care! I'll even go to a Baptist church from now on if that's what it takes! I love Larry so much and can't wait to marry him!'

Sarah nodded, looking down into the murky brown tea in her cup. Vivienne tilted her head.

'Sarah, aren't you happy for me?'

'Oh, yes! Of course I am. I'm sorry. I'm just so surprised! I'm worried what Mother will say to you.' Sarah paused thoughtfully. 'I hope it turns out well for you, Viv.'

Vivienne smiled.

'Thank-you, Sarah. Oh, I'm so happy!'

At her station, Sarah insured she was alone. Sitting at the desk, she turned to face the wall, covering her face with her hands. She closed her eyes and breathed deeply to control the flood of tears threatening to burst forth.

She had obeyed her mother's demand to not marry George, believing it would have made life too difficult for her. She had feared that the loneliness and inability to see her family would be too much to bear. But now Vivienne was going to marry a Baptist, facing the same prospect of alienation and yet she didn't care about it.

'What if Mother has changed her mind about marrying a non-Brethren, and everything turns out all right in the end?' Grace thought to herself. *'That would be so unfair for me. How could I ever forgive my mother?'*

The realization that survival was possible had come too late. She dreaded Vivienne's wedding day, when she would stand by and watch her sister marry the man she loved, knowing in her heart that if she had done the same with George, it would have been okay in the end for her too.

Chapter Thirteen

The waiting room was stark white and sterile. The telephone trilled, and the secretary recited a well-rehearsed greeting into the receiver. Sarah looked up at the clock hanging on the wall, her hands clasped tightly around her purse.

'Mrs. Brooker?' Dr. Webster stepped out of his office. 'How are you this morning?'

'Well, thank you, Doctor.'

She followed him into his office, sitting down opposite his desk.

'Well, Mrs. Brooker, I have good news for you!' he announced, holding up a piece of paper. 'You're pregnant, congratulations!'

'That's wonderful,' said Sarah with a half grin.

'I bet you can't wait to tell Jack.'

Sarah nodded. 'Oh, yes.'

Dr. Webster removed his glasses.

'Mrs. Brooker, I would have expected you to be a little more excited.'

'I am excited, Doctor,' Sarah assured. 'I am, of course. Forgive me; I'm just a little confused. Two months ago, you wrote me a prescription for the contraceptive pill.'

'Well, these things happen, don't they? After all, contraception isn't a guarantee that you won't fall pregnant.'

Sarah nodded.

'This has all happened very quickly. Jack and I have only been married for three months.'

'That is completely normal, Mrs. Brooker. Couples like you and Jack get married and have children all the time. That's how it goes.'

As the bus bumped along the road toward home, Sarah gazed pensively out the window. She had emerged from six years of dedicated study and an even longer standing ambition, and started her career barely a year ago. The timing of her first pregnancy was terrible in her overall plan.

Jack was ecstatic about becoming a father. Their church community showered the couple with congratulations, but behind Sarah's smile, panic simmered. Everything was happening so fast. Within a year she had married and fallen pregnant; how quickly her life had slipped out of her control. Discontentment festered within her rising panic; she'd always envisioned that her first pregnancy would be filled with joy, but joy evaded her. Maybe it was her fault, she thought. Maybe she had forgotten to take the pill one day.

Sarah continued to work for as long as the hospital permitted. Walking away from the hospital on her last day, she knew it would be a year or more before she could return.

That evening Sarah laid the dining table with two neatly ironed cloth napkins, bone handled cutlery, fine china plates and crystal glasses, items she had bought over her working years for her dowry.

'Look at me,' she thought. '*I look just like my mother, wearing an apron and doing housework.*'

With her first pregnancy she carried disappointment, yet in her private despair Sarah pledged to herself that she would make her situation work. She accepted the little being growing inside her and slipped into her homebound routine, having devised a new plan.

Autumn set in and the early mornings brought a chilly nip to the air. Each day, Sarah kissed Jack goodbye when he left for work, and then set about doing her housework so she could spend the afternoon doing her favourite hobbies, which included playing her piano, the family heirloom her mother had given to her. She also did intricate patterned knitting and hand embroidery. She was proud of her craft work. Like everything else, she did it to a high standard. Some days, Vivienne came out to visit after she had finished work at the hospital.

'Now, you sit down, Sarah,' Vivienne insisted, 'I'll make the tea.'

Sarah sat down at the kitchen table, leaning back in the chair and stroking her swollen belly. Vivienne filled the tin kettle and unscrewed the lid to the tealeaf jar.

'How are you feeling today?' she enquired, spooning the tealeaves into the ceramic pot.

Sarah sighed.

'Tired. I've never felt so tired in my life, not even from work. I'm not used to it at all.'

'Well, you make sure you look after yourself. Don't push yourself too hard.'

'I know, I just want to keep my mind busy. I'm just not used to being at home all day.'

Vivienne nodded.

'I can imagine it must be a big change from the hospital.'

The kettle began to whistle, and Vivienne removed it from the stove, pouring the water into the pot.

'So how are things at the hospital?' Sarah enquired.

'Oh, great,' Vivienne replied. 'Larry and I have been looking into doing missionary work too.'

'That sounds exciting,' said Sarah. 'I do hope I get to do something like that someday. I've mentioned it to Jack quite a few times, but his response has always been brief and dismissive.'

'Well, I can understand that. He will have a family to support soon.'

Vivienne waved her finger at Sarah.

'You just have that baby first.'

After Vivienne had gone, Sarah sat in the living room, thinking over her sister's news. Amidst all the events of the past year, she had almost forgotten her own dream of becoming a missionary. Now that she was married, she would only be allowed to undertake missionary work with her husband. Jack's enthusiasm was waning, but she still held onto hope that he would want to do it with her one day.

***

Sitting in the hospital waiting room, Jack resting his chin in his hand, his elbow balanced on his jiggling knee. He sighed, sitting back, clasping his hands together in his lap. There were two other men there, one reading a newspaper, the other sitting with his arms and legs crossed as he stared at the floor. They kept to themselves. Jack glanced occasionally at the clock on the wall. He stood up, casually pacing the room.

The doctor lifted a small, slippery body, his cries piercing the air. The warm body was placed on Sarah's chest, and she immediately forgot the pain of the preceding hours. The life that she had created inspired an enduring sense of power, and she felt like she could do anything. It was a moment even more special than her wedding, equalled by nothing else in her life.

Her baby boy was so fragile and precious, curled up on her chest seeking shelter from the bright light. His face was screwed up, his gummy mouth wide open as he cried.

He was taken away to be bathed and cleaned, and Sarah was wheeled to the maternity ward. There, her baby boy was returned to her, wrapped up tightly in a blanket. He looked up at her with big blue eyes, absorbing the new world around him. She stroked his cheek, the skin so soft and smooth. She had cradled many babies in her arms before, but this was so radically different to anything she'd ever experienced. This baby was hers.

She was proud and relieved that she had given birth to a boy as her eldest child. It would be well accepted in the family and in the church community. Jack arrived on the ward shortly after, smiling as he stroked their son's soft head with his calloused hand.

'I wish you could have been there,' said Sarah. 'I wish you could have felt as happy as I felt in that moment.'

64

Jack kissed her head.

'I'm just glad to have you back after all those hours. There were only so many cups of tea I could drink and biscuits I could eat.'

Each day after he finished work, Jack travelled to the hospital to visit Sarah and Paul. Shortly after his arrival one evening, a doctor paid the young family a visit.

'Mr. Brooker, I'm Doctor Norman. I'm a psychiatrist here at the hospital.'

'Psychiatrist?'

'Sarah's regular doctor has consulted with me about some concerns he has regarding Sarah's health. I was wondering if I could speak with you for a few minutes outside.'

Jack looked to Sarah, and then back at Dr. Norman.

'Alright,' he agreed, and followed him out of the room.

'Mr. Brooker, Sarah has not been sleeping well and is suffering from exhaustion. As a result, she is struggling to breastfeed. I've spoken with her privately, and she has shared with me that she is feeling anxious about taking Paul home and being alone with him.'

'Anxious?' Jack queried. 'Why would she feel that? She's a nurse. She handled babies all the time when she was at work.'

'Mr. Brooker, I have concerns for the baby's wellbeing if I sent them home now. I think it would be best if I extended their stay in hospital.'

Jack glanced back into the room at Sarah and Paul.

'I have noticed over the past few days that she seems worried about something. Though she hasn't mentioned anything to me.' Jack looked back at the doctor. 'How long will she have to stay?'

'I hope only a week or two. I've prescribed her with a low-strength anti-depressant whilst she's breastfeeding, which she may have to keep taking for some time. I want to make sure she is well adjusted before she is released from our care. Is there someone who can check on her at home throughout the day?'

'I guess her mother could. She lives on the other side of town, though.'

'Well, the medication along with plenty of rest is very important for her right now. We'll talk again in a few days.'

Two weeks after Paul's birth Sarah was released from hospital. Jack was glad to have them finally home; finally they could get on with their new life as a family.

The kookaburra's laugh erupted from the bush land next door, abruptly calling to attention sleepy and sluggish souls in the early hours of the morning. Their call was cheeky, and Sarah thought that it sounded as if the bird was laughing at the silly humans.

With Jack at work, Sarah paced the main bedroom, cooing to Paul as he cried and cried. She patted his back, bouncing him gently in her arms. She tried to feed him but could not stop him crying.

'I am a trained nurse,' she thought in frustration. *'I should be able to handle this situation!'*

Guilt fuelled her escalating panic. Why couldn't she satisfy her baby's needs? Why couldn't she understand what he was trying to tell her?

Tears blurred her vision as she searched her memory for answers. She leaned against the wall, sliding down to the floor with Paul in her arms. Squeezing her eyes closed, she sobbed aloud.

'Please stop,' she whimpered. 'Please be quiet.'

With Paul finally asleep in his crib, Sarah stepped up to the bathroom vanity and reached into the overhead cabinet. She took down a small bottle, unscrewed the lid and tipped a pill into her hand, swallowing it with a cup of water. She wanted so very much to balance motherhood and her career. She had waited this long; she could not fail in her plan. The turmoil she had gone through with her mother would have been for nothing. So she was

determined to get through this phase of her life and make her plan
work.

Chapter Fourteen

Jack arrived home from work just after four o'clock. Paul was sleeping in his crib, and Sarah stood before the bedroom mirror in her uniform, adjusting the white cap on her head. It had been almost a year, but the time had finally come. She had secured a part-time job working several nights a week at a nursing home. She could hardly wait to step back into her duties.

'Sarah, the taxi's here,' Jack whispered, sticking his head into the room.

Sarah picked up her bag and met Jack at the door.

'Paul's bottle is in the refrigerator. Just warm the milk before you feed him. Make sure it's not too hot.'

'Alright,' Jack nodded. 'I'll be fine. Have a good first night back.'

Sarah arrived home in the early hours of the morning, crawling into bed and sleeping for a few hours until Paul woke again, and the daily routine started once more. Sarah's days were kept busy attending to Paul's needs and doing the housework, and occasionally she would rest in the afternoon while Paul was sleeping. She cooked dinner, and when Jack returned home, she left for work. By the time she made it to church on Sunday, she was so tired she could barely keep her eyes open.

Since she had left the hospital, she had devised a plan for how she would get back to work after her pregnancy. There was no other option for her; she had to be a success. She didn't even want to give a moment's thought to the possibility of not being able to do what she loved. But her body was fighting against her, and she didn't know how long she could continue to battle against it.

***

Bouncing Paul on her lap, Sarah found herself once again in Dr. Webster's office.

'Congratulations, Mrs. Brooke. A baby brother or sister for little Paul!'

Sarah looked down at her son, stroking his hair.

'Here we go again,' she whispered.

'Is anything the matter, Mrs. Brooker?'

'Well, it's just that, it's only been five months since Paul was born. I feel like I've only just recovered.'

'You've returned to work, haven't you?'

'Yes, just night shifts at a nursing home.'

'Well, that explains your fatigue and weight loss.' Dr. Webster paused thoughtfully. 'I don't think you should be working during this pregnancy, Mrs. Brooker. If your health deteriorates, you could lose this baby. You really must take it easy.'

Ryan was born in the spring of 1959, and Sarah was allowed home without a prolonged stay in hospital. Sarah managed to care for the boys by herself during the day and, after a few months, she returned to her night shifts at work. Ryan and Paul were the pride of her and Jack's lives, and they shared many happy memories together as a family. Sarah kept her head held high. Her overall health had been better during her second pregnancy, and she had not suffered the emotional peril she'd faced before and after Paul's birth.

Sarah was expecting again by Ryan's first birthday and carried her third baby through the hot and sticky Queensland summer. As her third pregnancy progressed, her health depleted. Depressed and overtired, she took her medication the way Dr. Webster had prescribed.

In March, Sarah gave birth to a girl. It was a pleasant surprise to have a daughter, and Grace was Sarah's own little delight. She daydreamed of the times when Grace was older, when she could take her shopping in the city for pretty dresses and spend mother and daughter time chatting over tea in city cafes.

Sarah cut back her nursing shifts when she returned to work after Grace was six months old. However, as it was before, Sarah's balancing act was soon tipped off kilter, and she found herself back in Dr Webster's office.

'Sarah, I'm very worried for your welfare,' Dr Webster stated. 'You have three children under the age of five. You can't continue to push yourself the way you are. You will quickly burn out, and it would take you a long time to recover, even longer seeing as you have to look after your children.'

Sarah remembered the day long ago when she had started her nursing training. She had been so happy and excited, but now those memories brought about only sadness. She felt she had barely had the chance to start her career before she had been left with no choice but to give it up.

Walking away from her job and colleagues at the nursing home, in her despair Sarah clung to a thin glimmer of hope. Her dream had been delayed for the time being, but one day when the children were older, she was determined she would return to her career.

Sarah looked down at Grace as she slept in her crib. Her emotions were a mixture of love and frustration.

'If only I hadn't fallen pregnant so soon, I would be going to work tonight.'

Sarah positioned Ryan in his highchair and Paul in the seat next to her at the dining table. Jack prayed for the meal, and they began to eat, and Sarah filled teaspoons of mashed vegetables and fed them to the boys.

'I received a letter from Vivienne today.'

'I see,' said Jack, pushing meat and vegetables onto his fork. 'How do they like living in Mackay?'

'She said it has been a great experience so far.'

'I'm sure it has been,' Jack agreed.

Sarah looked thoughtfully at her husband.

'Jack, I know I've said this many times over, but I really would love for us to get involved in church missionary work. I would love to do something like that with you, Jack.'

Jack looked up at her.

'We are busy enough as it is, Sarah. We've got a newborn baby. And besides, I'm busy as a leader in the church already. I work all week and on Saturday's I help build the church building and landscaping the grounds. If I am not at work, I am at the church.'

After dinner Sarah picked Ryan and Paul up out of their chairs and put them to bed. She returned to the kitchen, where Jack was washing the dishes. She vigorously dried the plates and placing them on the shelves. Jack stopped washing.

'Sarah, what's wrong?' He tilted his head thoughtfully, turning to her. 'Is it because I said I don't want to become a missionary?'

She stopped, resting one hand on her hip. She didn't look up at him, desperately trying to keep from crying. Jack approached her, placing his hand on her shoulder.

'I'm sorry, Sarah. My missionary work is here in Brisbane at our church. You're my wife, Sarah, I need your support.' He sighed. 'You've had a long day. Go and sit down. I'll take care of the dishes.'

Jack brought the cup of tea to Sarah in her armchair.

'You know, sweetie, even if I wanted to be an overseas missionary, with your health could you handle missionary work anyway? You have a tough enough time as it is.'

Chapter Fifteen

Jack paced in the waiting room, frequently glancing at the door awaiting any news. Sarah was currently in surgery undergoing an emergency caesarean section. She had not been well during her fourth pregnancy. Her high blood pressure had been causing problems. After what seemed like an eternity, Jack was reunited with Sarah, who was holding a healthy baby boy.

Vivienne and her husband Larry had moved from Mackay back to Brisbane. Sarah was glad to have her sister close by again; she had struggled through her pregnancy with Daniel. Yet despite Vivienne's return, Sarah's depression continued, and Jack decided to take her back to see Dr. Norman at the hospital.

'How long has this been going on for?' asked Dr. Norman.

'Six months,' said Sarah. 'Since Daniel was born.'

'This has been going on for too long, and it's not getting better like we'd hoped it would. This is too much for you to handle on your own under the care of your local doctor. I would like to re-admit you to hospital for some psychiatric evaluation and rest.'

'Back to hospital?' Sarah repeated.

Dr. Norman nodded.

'It is important that you're admitted as soon as possible.'

Sarah didn't speak on the way home. Jack glanced over at her, noting the trouble in her eyes.

'Talk to me, sweetheart,' he urged.

'How could I be such a failure as a mother?' she asked.

'You're not a failure, Sarah. You're not. You're just having a difficult time, that's all.' He took one hand from the wheel and placed it over Sarah's. 'You'll get through this. You will.'

They arrived at The Grange to pick up the children, and Jack requested to speak with his father in private.

'I know this is extremely short notice, Dad, but I need to take a week off work to get Sarah off to hospital and organize myself to look after the kids while she's away.'

Clayton shook his head.

'You can't stop working because your wife has problems.'

'Well, maybe Mum and Aileen can take turns in looking after them while I am at work. They'd enjoy that, surely.'

'No, Jack. You have a six-month-old baby; that is too much to ask of your mother and poor Aileen. What about Sarah's sisters?'

'They all have their own families to look after. And they work.'

'Well, you'll have to figure something out, Jack. I can give you two days. That's all. This is your problem, Jack. You need to sort it out. It is not up to others to shoulder your burden.' Clayton paused. 'You should put the kids in the children's home until Sarah comes out of hospital. Then you can get on with work and focusing on supporting your family.'

Standing in the living room, Sarah held Daniel close to her chest, cradling his precious little head in her hand. She passed Daniel to her mother and knelt in front of the three older children, fiercely holding back the tears with her smile.

'Kids, you remember what we talked about? Mummy must go away for a little while. I'll see you again very soon, alright?'

Paul and Ryan nodded. Sarah looked tenderly at two-year-old Grace, stroked her daughter's round cheek with her thumb. She gathered all three children into her embrace, holding them close and kissing their heads.

'I love you all so much,' she whispered.

'Sweetheart, we should get going,' Jack said quietly, holding her suitcase.

Sarah nodded, pulling back and briskly wiping the tear from her cheek with her hand. She took a deep breath as she stood up and followed Jack out the front door. She stepped out onto the front porch, hearing Paul start to whimper. Ryan quickly joined in, and then Grace.

'Now, now, children. Let Mummy go,' Aileen soothed.

'Mummy!' they howled. 'Mummy!'

'Come on, Sarah,' Jack urged. 'Come on.'

Sarah covered her mouth with her hand, lowering her head, sheltering her quiet sobs under her breath. Jack whispered comfort to her as he carefully guided her down the driveway to the car.

Jack pulled up outside the plain white building, waiting there for a few moments. Looking out the window, he pondered driving away right then and there. With his father's voice in his head, he stepped out of the car. Holding Daniel in his arms, he walked with the children into the building. Inside, they were greeted by the matron.

'You must be Jack Brooker?'

'Yes,' Jack replied.

'I am Sister Stanley.'

'This is Paul, Ryan, and Grace. 'Jack placed his free hand on the heads of the three older children as he introduced them. 'And this here is Daniel.'

Sister Stanley nodded.

'Well, Mr. Brooker, I assure you we will take good care of them here. Now, visiting times are a few hours on the weekend. You must stay here with them during that time.'

'Can't I take them out for the day?'

'No. You must stay here. It makes things easier for them while they're away from home. We don't want their routine being disrupted.'

Jack knelt before his children.

'Now, kids, you're going to be staying here for a little while. I'll come and visit you in a few days and we'll spend some time together.'

'Daddy, why can't we go with you?' Paul cried.

'I'll see you soon,' Jack assured him. 'You'll be alright. You have Grace and Ryan here with you, and I need you to be brave for them. Sister Stanley here will take good care of all of you.'

Jack stood up and passed Daniel into Sister Stanley's waiting arms. He turned to leave, the sound of his children's cries was like daggers in his back as he walked toward the exit.

'*Don't turn back, Jack,*' he thought to himself. '*Don't turn back.*'

'Daddy! Daddy!'

'Settle down now, children!' Sister Stanley commanded. 'Settle down!'

'Daddy! Please come back!'

The children's cries were swiftly shut out as the door swung closed behind him. Jack continued to the car and sat in the driver's seat. He exhaled sharply, placing his hands on the steering wheel, tightening his grip around it, taking deep breaths. He wanted so badly to run back inside, scoop them up in his arms and take them away. He could barely comprehend only seeing them once a week, and who knew how long it would be before they could come home?

Jack gathered himself, clearing his throat and drying his eyes. He turned the key in the ignition, pulling the car out into the street.

Jack visited Sarah in the hospital every afternoon after work. The house was too quiet. At six o'clock, he turned on the bedside radio and listened to the news until he fell asleep. He often woke throughout the night thinking he'd heard Daniel crying, only to remember that the house was empty.

On Sunday morning, Jack sat with his mother in the first pew at church. Before them, Clayton delivered his sermon from the pulpit. In his whole life Jack had never felt so embarrassed. The absence of Sarah and the children would certainly raise questions.

Since Paul's birth, the church community had known of Sarah's emotional struggles. Each Sunday they passed on their well wishes to him before quickly changing the subject. They preferred to avoid the details and only engage in light-hearted conversation.

In the hospital, Sarah felt as if she had been plucked from her real life, and placed into a nightmare, where the hours dragged, and the days blurred into one. The only time that mattered in there was the time of a doctor's appointment, mealtimes and Jack's daily visit.

Sarah yearned to hold her children, and to nurse little Daniel in her arms. She felt their absence like an amputated limb. She missed Jack; the visits were never long enough, and the time between them was unbearable. She wanted him close so she wouldn't feel afraid or sad anymore, so she would know everything would be all right. Just to have him by her side to hold her hand.

The first month spilled over into the next. Dr. Norman visited Sarah daily, asking her questions and scribbling notes onto his clipboard. Nurses brought her pills with a cup of water, and on and on it went. The second month ticked over into the third, and still the nurses came with their pills, and Dr. Norman with his notes. One day, just when Sarah had given up hope that she would ever leave, Dr. Norman brought with him good news; he had deemed her fit to return home.

Standing by her hospital bed, Sarah folded her clothes and placed them in her suitcase. She looked up, smiling as Jack came into the room.

'Jack!' she beamed.

He embraced her.

'Are you ready to go?'

'Yes,' Sarah replied.

The Austin utility was parked outside the hospital entrance. Jack placed Sarah's suitcase behind the seats and climbed into the driver's seat beside her. He reached over and took her hand.

'We'll pick the kids up together. They'll be so excited to see you.'

'I can't wait to see them. I've missed them so much.'

They arrived at the home, and Sister Stanley brought the children out to meet them.

'Mummy!' they cried. 'Mummy!'

Sarah dropped to her knees as they came running into her embrace. She smothered their faces with kisses, squeezing them all so tightly she felt she might crush them with love. She stood up and took Daniel in her arms, rocking him gently. That spot in her heart where she always held him had been so cold and empty.

'I will never leave you again!' she cried. 'I promise I will never leave you again!'

Chapter Sixteen

In the seaside suburb of Redcliffe, half an hour's drive north of Brisbane, Jack and Clayton found a waterfront property for sale to use as a holiday home for their family, and for the church to use for occasional weekend camps. It was a single level house with fibro walls and a tin roof, and a lockup garage out the front of the house. There were two-bedrooms with a spacious front room that faced the ocean. Jack filled it with second-hand furniture. He put four sets of bunk beds along the length of the front room, as well as two single beds that served as couches. He and Clayton built bunk beds around the walls of the garage to provide ample bedding for the weekend campers.

In the kitchen a gas stove sat in the recess where its wood-fired predecessor had once been. The kitchen had a free-standing pantry. Sarah did not bring any of her fine china to the holiday house in fear they would get broken when the church congregation used the house.

There was an upward sliding window beside the sink, and the kids often used it as a secret entrance to the house. The laundry was located under an easement outside the back door. When Sarah had laundry to do, she wheeled the old round washing tub over to the concrete sink against the laundry wall. She pulled the long extension arm of the tap over to the machine and filled it with water, then loaded in the dirty clothes and flicked the switch on the side. She set a kitchen timer for five minutes, and when it buzzed, the children came running to help her. The children loved to wring out the clothes before they were hung on the Hills Hoist clothesline. Careful not to get their fingers caught, one child fed the piece of clothing through the two rollers on the machine, and another would catch the garment as it came through the other end, stiff as a board. The kids laughed and laughed; it was just like in the Road Runner cartoon when the character Wile E. Coyote got squashed on the road from being run over by a car.

It was the May Day long weekend, and Jack had barely pulled up outside the holiday house as the kids spilled out of the car.

'We're here!' they squealed.

Sarah laughed, sitting Daniel on her hip. The kids ran excitedly straight to the front yard.

'Dad's the tides in, can we go for a swim?' Paul yelled as they ran back to the car.

'Yes, we can after you help me take everything from the car inside.'

The beach was rocky with only a small amount of sand. Jack had built a boat ramp so they could launch their dinghy, and it was only at high tide that they could swim out the front of their house. Jack would always join the kids, while Sarah preferred to watch from the front yard. At low tide, she sat on the rocks with Daniel in her arms as the older children played on the sand.

Before Jack would take the children fishing, they would go digging for worms at low tide on what they called 'worm island' out the front of the house. Jack would dig and the children would watch in readiness to grab the worms before they dug back into the rocks. When a worm was spotted, Sarah could hear them from the house yelling with excitement.

As the long weekend drew to a close, Jack and the children scrambled to savour the last moments of their holiday. After lunch on Monday, Jack launched his old tin dinghy. Fishing was his favourite pastime, and he loved to take Paul, Ryan and Grace out in the boat with him.

'Bye, Mummy!' the children shouted out as they puttered away from the beach.

'Bye!' Sarah called back, waving to them from the foreshore. 'Have fun! Catch lots of fish!'

'We will!'

Jack puttered the boat half an hour to the Hornibrook Bridge, where he turned the engine off and helped the children with their fishing rods. Holding her rod over the side of the boat, Grace felt a sharp tug on the line.

'Dad! Dad!' She shrieked. 'I got one!'

Jack moved quickly to sit beside her, guiding her hands as she wound the reel. The fish appeared up through the water into the air, and in her excitement, Grace stood to her feet, the fish swinging around in circles over their heads on the end of the fishing line. Jack grappled for the line, bringing the situation under control, laughing all the while.

They returned later in the afternoon, and Jack packed up the car. Soon after they'd hit the road the children were sound asleep. When they arrived back in Keperra, Sarah took Daniel inside while Jack woke the older children. They whined as they stirred, wandering half asleep up to the house and collapsing into their beds. Sarah pulled their blankets up over them, softly kissing their foreheads. She went into the main bedroom and leaned over into Daniel's crib, gently touching his stomach as he slept soundly on his back. She turned to the bed and lay down next to Jack, rolling onto her side to face him.

'Thank you for another wonderful weekend,' she whispered.

'It was great, wasn't it? There is many more of them to come.' Jack yawned.

Sarah peeled her eyes open, squinting as she gazed sleepily around the dark bedroom. A strange sound was coming from the other side of the room. She sat up and stood quickly to her feet, approaching Daniel's crib. Vomit was dribbling down his chin. She quickly picked him up, taking him into the bathroom and grabbing a towel. While she nursed him in the living room, Jack cleaned up the cot.

Daniel's vomiting eased, and Sarah was able to rock him back to sleep. She lay him down in the crib; it wasn't long before Daniel's sickness called her up again.

'What could be making him sick?' Jack asked.

'A virus, perhaps.' Sarah sighed, shaking her head. 'I hope the other kids haven't caught it.'

'I'll call the doctor first thing in the morning and get him to come by the house to look at Daniel,' said Sarah.

Sitting on Sarah's lap, Daniel cried out and squirmed as Dr. Webster pressed the cold head of the stethoscope against his chest. Dr. Webster reached into his black leather bag and took out a thermometer, which he placed under Daniel's chubby arm, leaving it there for several minutes.

'Well, he's got a temperature,' Dr. Webster stated as he inspected the thermometer. 'I suspect he has Tonsillitis.'

Sarah brushed her hand over Daniel's soft hair. Dr. Webster took a small bottle of medicine out of his bag.

'Give him one teaspoon every four hours. Call me if you have any further problems.'

'Alright,' Sarah nodded. 'Thank you for coming out.'

'It was no trouble at all,' Dr Webster replied as he clicked his bag closed.

After work, Jack travelled back to his parents' house with his father.

'Have you heard from Sarah, Mum?'

'Yes, this morning. She said the doctor thinks it is Tonsillitis. He gave her some medicine to give Daniel.'

Jack nodded.

'I won't stay for a cuppa. I'll get home and see how Sarah is coping with Daniel. She hardly got any sleep last night.'

When Jack arrived home, he greeted Sarah with a kiss on the cheek.

'How's Daniel?'

'He's been asleep for hours. I managed to catch up on my sleep as well.'

Jack walked up to the crib, looked at the colour of his face, picking him up.

'Sarah, his body is limp!' Jack exclaimed.

'What?' Sarah gasped. 'Oh, my goodness.'

'Call a cab. I'll stay home with the kids; you take him to hospital right now.'

Paul and Ryan came running to the lounge room where Jack was talking urgently to his mother on the telephone.

'What's wrong Daddy?'

Sarah nervously packed a change of clothes and some toiletries just in case she had to stay overnight at the hospital.

Grace peered into her parent's bedroom.

'Mummy?'

'Not now Grace.'

When the taxi arrived, Jack walked out to the car with Sarah, who carried Daniel wrapped up in a blanket. He opened the door, and she slipped down into the back seat.

'Everything's going to be alright, love,' he insisted, closing the door and watching the taxi drive off down the road.

After dinner, Jack bathed Paul, Ryan and Grace and then put them to bed. He cleaned up the kitchen, and then sat in his armchair in the living room. His mind was awash with worry. A clock sat on top of a glass cabinet. The slow tick-tock tormented him as he waited for the phone to ring. The hands read eight o'clock. He watched the occasional set of headlights flash by on the road outside, but none of them stopped.

He frequently nodded off to sleep, but quickly woke each time. He didn't want to go to sleep until he knew everything was all right with Daniel and Sarah.

The phone rang at eleven, startling Jack out of his doze. It was Sarah; she was calling from a payphone.

'How is everything going?' Jack enquired.

'Daniel is settled. He has been placed in a special ward. The doctors don't know what's wrong with him yet. They are going to do further tests tomorrow.'

Jack exhaled heavily.

'That's good news.'

'I wanted to stay with him tonight, but the nurses are insisting I go home. I'm about to call a taxi, so I will be home soon.'

'Alright. I'll wait up for you.'

Jack checked on the children and then returned to his armchair, where he dozed off again. The phone rang and he woke again with a start.

'Hello?'

'Jack Brooker?'

'Yes.'

'This is the Head Nurse from the Children's Ward. You and your wife had better come back to the hospital straight away. Daniel has deteriorated very quickly.'

Jack's heart sank.

'Sarah was just there. She's on her way home.'

'As soon as she gets home, you should come back to the hospital immediately.'

Jack hung up and dialled his parents straight away.

'Dad, its Jack. Daniel is in the hospital; he's got a virus or something. He's really bad...'

'Jack, slow down!'

'Sarah is on her way home, as soon as she gets back, we have to go into the hospital again. Could you please come and watch the kids for us?'

'Alright. We'll come over straight away.'

'Thank you so much, Dad.'

Jack collapsed back down in the armchair again, dropping his head in his hand.

'Please God,' he prayed aloud, 'Please hear me! Please, help us now! Please take care of Daniel, and please bring Sarah home quickly! Please, God!'

He stood and paced the living room, looking out the window. Finally, he saw headlights slow and stop. He met Sarah at the door.

'The hospital rang. We must go back there. Daniel has deteriorated.'

'What?' Sarah gasped. 'I was just there!'

'I know, but they called just after you'd left. I've phoned my parents and they're on their way here to watch the kids.'

Jack helped Sarah sit down on the couch, holding her hands.

'I was just there!' Sarah exclaimed, shaking her head. 'I wanted to stay but they insisted I go home! He looked fine when I left! He was fast asleep! His temperature was fine! How could this happen so quickly?'

She looked at Jack.

'When we go back there, I'm staying with him until he comes home! I won't leave him this time!'

'Alright,' Jack soothed. 'That's good. You do that. I'll be okay here.'

Sarah rested her head on his shoulder, and he held her close. Clayton and Dot arrived, and Jack and Sarah hurried down to the utility parked in the backyard garage. Jack turned the key in the ignition, and the engine choked and splattered.

'Come on!' Jack growled. 'Come on!'

'What's wrong, Jack?'

'The battery is dead!'

They jumped out of his utility again.

'What happened?' Clayton called from the back steps.

'The battery is dead,' Jack replied. 'Can we take your car?'

'Yes, of course,' Clayton replied, tossing down the keys.

Finally, Jack and Sarah were on their way. The headlights lit the dirt road a short distance ahead through the darkness. They arrived in the city, and Jack had barely pulled up at the main entrance to the hospital when Sarah pushed open the door and ran inside to the reception. Jack parked the utility and ran back to Sarah. Pushing through the double doors, he spotted Sarah at the desk. He hurried to her side, catching his breath as he looked from Sarah to the nurse.

'You said he was okay!' Sarah yelled. 'You people said he was okay! That's why I went home! You told me to go home!'

'I'm so sorry, Mrs. Brooker. He was fine when you left; he turned very suddenly.'

Sarah's legs buckled underneath her, and Jack lurched forward to catch her, and nurses hurried to help them as he guided Sarah to sit on a chair. Containing her explosive grief in his embrace, Jack broke down as he tried to comfort her.

'Daniel!' Sarah wailed. 'Daniel!'

Chapter Seventeen

Grace wandered down the hallway half asleep, her favourite doll tucked under her arm. She found her father in the kitchen with her brothers.

'Daniel has gone up to the sky to be with God,' he explained to the boys, pointing out the window.

Grace's little heart was flooded with disappointment.

'Why didn't you wake me Daddy so I could see Daniel fly up to the sky?'

'Is he coming back?' Paul asked.

Jack shook his head.

'No, son.'

'Why not?' Ryan persisted. 'Why can't he come back to us?'

'Because God wants Daniel to live with Him now.'

'Why would God take him away from us? This is his home. We are his family. God gave Daniel to us and now he wants him back? That's not fair!'

In the bedroom, Sarah lay on her side, the sheets tangled around her body. Her gaze was fixated on her reflection in the dressing table mirror across the way. In the corner, the crib stood empty and silent. Daniel had been there not twelve hours ago.

'I should have saved him,' she thought. *'I'm a nurse. I should have known what was wrong. I should have known to stay with him. Why did I leave my sick son?'*

Later in the morning, Clayton and Dot came around to check on the family. They sat with Jack at the kitchen table, and Dot made tea.

'It was a brain flu,' said Jack. 'They say that if he'd survived it, he would have severe mental disability.

'Oh, Jack,' Dot soothed.

'It was God's will,' said Clayton. 'Think of what it would have been like if he had lived. Caring for him in that state, the miserable life he would have had. Sarah can barely cope with the kids you already have, let alone one with brain damage.'

Dot poured the tea and placed the cups in front of Jack and Clayton.

'I just don't know what to say to the kids. I don't think they really understand what has happened, that Daniel isn't coming back. Maybe the funeral will help it make sense to them.'

'You shouldn't take the children to the funeral,' said Clayton.

'Why not?' asked Jack.

'It's not appropriate, Jack. They're too young. It will be too much, seeing people crying. You need to be there for Sarah, so she holds it together. She will need you. That will be enough for you to deal with on the day, let alone children as well.'

Jack screwed up his face, trying to block out the words of his father, his emotions slipping erratically between from anger to deep sorrow and panic.

'Now, now, son,' Clayton warned. 'You mustn't cry, you understand? You can't fall apart like Sarah. You need to be strong and support your family.'

Jack swallowed hard, fiercely blinking back the tears burning behind his eyes. He lowered his head, finding his vision blurry as the tears threatened to escape despite his best efforts. Dot reached over and touched his arm.

'God will heal your sorrows, Jack.'

'Don't take the children to the funeral,' Clayton demanded.

Jack's alarm clock rang on the bedside table, and he dragged himself out of bed. Standing in front of the bathroom mirror, his reflection was drained of life. His mind was numb, his actions were mechanical as he showered and shaved.

Back in the bedroom, from the wardrobe he took the suit he wore to church every week. With trembling hands, he looped his tie through the knots. He never imagined that he would be wearing the same suit to the funeral of his own child.

Daniel's coffin was draped in an embroidered white cloth at the front of the chapel, with an arrangement of flowers resting on top. Sitting hand in hand with her husband, Sarah thought that maybe this was all just a terrible dream. Maybe she would wake up soon, overwhelmed with enormous relief to see Daniel sleeping in his crib in the corner of their bedroom. She would laugh with delight at his cry, lovingly lift him and hold him until he calmed. Surely something like this could not be real. How could she endure this if it were?

The coffin was so small; she had never seen anything like it. The very concept of a baby-sized coffin made her feel ill. The very need for its existence in the world seemed so wrong. An adult's casket symbolized the end of a life. Even if the person had met an untimely death, it left behind the remembrance of memories and legacies. One could find peace as they honoured the achievements of the deceased. Everything about the coffin before them that day symbolized pure tragedy, and reflection only induced further grief over the life cut short after only nine months. Sarah pressed her handkerchief to her mouth in a desperate attempt to contain her sobs. It was unacceptable behaviour to cry uncontrollably in their church community.

Clayton stepped up behind the pulpit at the front of the church to lead the funeral service.

'Friends, thank you for joining us today to comfort Sarah and Jack in the loss of their son, Daniel. Our prayers are with you and your children in this difficult time.'

As Jack listened to his father speak, his religious life played in his mind like a film. Nothing made sense to him as he sat there in the chapel he'd attended for years. Jack felt angry at God; it seemed as if God had turned his back on them and was punishing them.

'What did we do wrong to deserve this punishment?' he thought.

***

After that day, every time that he returned to the church, he would see the structure that had hosted his son's funeral. Nevertheless, next week he would be expected to come back and worship as he always had.

After the service, the guests gathered outside for morning tea. Sarah's friend Amelia touched her arm, shaking her head.

'We're so sorry, Sarah. We couldn't even start to understand what you're going through. It was a brain flu that took him, wasn't it?'

Sarah nodded. 'They say that if he'd survived it, he would have suffered severe mental handicap.

'Oh, Sarah,' Amelia soothed. 'Think of what that would have been to endure. Imagine caring for him in that state, and the miserable life it would have been for you and him.'

Sarah was sick of hearing that line. How many times people had told her that over the past week.

As he drove home Jack was lost in his own thoughts.

'How will Sarah ever be able to cope with this', he wondered. *'How will I manage with her not well, and feeling like I can't cope, when we still need to care for the kids?'*

Sarah looked out her window as they pulled into the driveway. Most of the flowers on the rose bush in the garden, at the far end of the front yard, had wilted and died, and only a single blossom remained amongst the leaves. Its petals were wilted too, and it had lost its lively, red colouring and full shape, drooping toward the ground. It too was dying.

Mrs. Williams, the Brooker's next-door neighbour, was reading a book to the children in the living room.

'What happened at the funeral?' Paul asked curiously.

Sarah said nothing, passing by them and walking down the hall to the bedroom, closing the door. Jack looked back at his son.

'We'll talk about it later, Paul,' he sighed. 'Thank you for watching the kids, Mrs. Williams.'

'No trouble, Jack. I've cooked a casserole. It's in the oven ready to eat.'

Jack mindlessly walked into the kitchen, taking plates from the shelves. He served up the casserole and placed a plate in front of each child at the table.

'Where's Mummy?' asked Paul.

'She isn't feeling well,' Jack replied. 'We'll just let her sleep tonight, okay?'

The sun came up on the second morning after Daniel's death. While Jack made breakfast for the children, Sarah stayed in bed. The final blow had been dealt, and she simply could not fathom the motivation to get up one more time.

Troubles had plagued her since she was eleven years old. All along, she had done what she'd thought was the right thing in the eyes of her family and her religion. She had given up the man she had loved with all her heart, only to watch not only Vivienne but Hilary as well go on to marry Baptist men. Bridget had gone one step further and wed a non-Christian.

Sarah had watched Vivienne achieve everything that she had wanted for herself, while she lost her career and good health as a result of having four children in five years; she had suffered depression and fatigue all along the way and finally the losing her baby child.

Once upon a time, she had been a confident, determined young woman. An A-grade student, a high achiever in school sports, an accomplished pianist and a fully qualified Nursing Sister, who had been reduced to housewife and motherly duties by her poor health. She had watched her sister and her friends continue their nursing careers, and then to lose a child in infancy was too much for her to bear.

The door was open slightly, and Paul, Ryan, and Grace stood together outside in the hallway, peeking through the gap.

'Mummy?' Paul called softly. 'Are you getting up this

morning?'

They waited, but there was no answer. Jack heard their soft voices from the kitchen. They were like three little angels standing there. He came down the hall to join them.

'Come on, kids,' he said quietly. 'Let Mummy rest. She'll get up later when I go to work.'

Driving along the dirt road, Jack stared blankly out the windscreen. Despite it all, he reasoned with himself that it was probably for the best that he went back to work so soon. If he didn't, he feared that the sadness would surely overwhelm him too, and he wouldn't be able to look after his family. Grief was tearing him apart from the inside out, but he needed to be strong. So, with his chin up, he kept driving.

Aileen helped Sarah and her grandchildren, and Vivienne and the rest of Sarah's family did what they could to support Sarah and Jack through the difficult time. Over the weeks, Sarah listened disinterested to the condolences from many well-meaning friends and relatives, who profusely reminded her that if she trusted God, her pain would be relieved.

Her sadness was more than she thought anyone else, even Jack or Vivienne, could possibly understand. Jack tried to comfort her and help her get well again. Vivienne sat and cried with her sister, but she and Jack quickly realized that Sarah had closed off to everyone. Jack took her back to Dr. Norman in search of help and answers, but all they came away with was a prescription for Valium.

In time, the rawness of grief eased for all but one member of the Brooker family, and life gradually returned to some resemblance of normality. Vivienne and her husband and children set off on another missionary adventure to Papua New Guinea, and although Sarah received several letters from her sister, the separation only added to her struggles.

Paul, Ryan and Grace were full of energy and mischief, and Jack formed a close bond with them as they grew. After finding himself alone most of the time in his parental role, he relied on the teachings of his religion to bring order into a difficult situation. He had decided his household would adhere strictly to the church teaching, and they would not deviate from them. With that decision Jack felt confident he could keep his household running smoothly. He firmly disciplined his children, but he was also fair, loving and gentle.

Read Grace's poem 'My Baby Brother' in Part 4

Part Three
The Wilted Rose

Chapter Eighteen

In August, the lights, sounds, and excitement of the Royal Brisbane Exhibition came to the RNA show grounds. Jack took the children every year. Wrapped up in their warm winter clothes, they wandered through Sideshow Alley as the chilling westerly winds howled through the laneways. The children enjoyed a few amusement rides, and stallholders called to them to try their game for the chance to win a prize.

The show bags were good value for money. In the honey sample bag were small packets of honey and small pieces of honeycomb. They always bought the liquorice bag. There were also various chip, lolly and chocolate bags to be had. Once they had their sample bags, the children patiently followed Jack around while he looked at the machinery and hardware displays. It was boring, but they were occupied with their sample bags and their bag of cheerios and tomato sauce and the promise of a strawberry ice cream.

As the sun began to set over the show grounds, Jack bought the children toasted sandwiches to eat as they settled into the main arena, to watch the fireworks erupt into an explosive display of colours once nightfall arrived.

'Dad, they look like big flowers!' Grace exclaimed.

After the explosions ceased, the air was silent and still, the colours faded, leaving drizzles of smoke against the night sky. Jack made sure the children gathered their now half empty show bags, and then they followed the rest of the crowd out of the arena.

'Dad?' asked Grace.

'Yes, Grace?'

'Why didn't Mummy come with us?'

Jack brushed his hand over her brown bob of hair.

'She isn't feeling well, sweetie.'

Grace looked down at the ground pouting.

'She's never feeling well. She never does anything with us.'

'When she is well, she does things with you.' Jack wrapped his arm around her. 'We're having fun, aren't we?'

'Yes,' Grace smiled.

A few months later, on the fifth of November, the fireworks returned. Jack walked the children to the corner store, where they bought a mixture of fireworks and crackers. After dinner, they followed Jack down to the back fence.

'Dad, I want a whizzer!' Ryan cried.

'I want a rocket!' Paul added.

Grace didn't like the big bangers, instead choosing the pretty spinning wheel. Jack hammered the wheel onto one of the wooden posts that held up the diamond mesh back fence. Paul and Ryan put bungers under tin cans, watching them explode and fly up into the sky.

As the children yelled and squealed in delight, Jack looked behind him to the stone retainer wall. There stood Sarah, smiling down at them.

'Mum! Come down and watch!' Ryan shouted.

Sarah followed the path alongside the wall and stood with Jack. They could hear the distant bangs from the crackers in the neighbouring backyards, seeing the colours shoot up over the treetops. Jack slipped his hand around Sarah's.

'Dad! Mum! Watch this one!'

'I'm watching, Paul.' Sarah said.

***

Once a month Sarah gathered herself together enough to make the trip into the city centre. The outings were an excursion for her and the children, an adventure beyond their isolated suburb.

'Paul, hold still!' Sarah instructed as she combed his hair.

'Sorry, Mum,' Paul giggled. 'You're very happy today!'

'Yes, I am, darling. We're going to have a lovely day out in the city.'

She patted Paul on the shoulder.

'Right, you're done. Ryan, come in here please!'

When Ryan was dressed and his hair combed, Sarah turned her attention to Grace. Grace sat up on the edge of her bed, while her mother buckled her shoes.

'Mummy, can I take my doll?'

'Alright,' Sarah agreed. 'Just make sure you don't lose her.'

Dressed in their very best outfits, Sarah took the children out into the yard and stood them in front of the house, holding the box brownie camera steady.

'Alright kids, smile!' She took the picture, and then lowered the camera in her hands, winding it on. 'Lovely.'

They crossed the road and walked down the adjacent street to the bus stop. When the bus arrived, the kids ran ahead down the aisle as Sarah paid the driver with coins for their tickets. The boys clambered onto a seat of their own, and Grace sat in front of them, waiting for her mother. The bus wound its way through the suburban streets all the way into the city.

The children followed Sarah around as she paid the household bills at the relevant offices. Afterwards, they shopped for clothes in Myers and Penny's department stores. The children were always so excited seeing so many people walking about, cars rushing by and the trams that rattled along the middle of Queen Street.

When they had finished their shopping, Sarah took them to the cafeteria above Penny's department store where they ate ham and cheese sandwiches for lunch.

As Grace munched away at her sandwich, she watched as her mother propped her handbag up on her lap, fishing out a small paper sachet. She tipped the aspirin powder from the sachet into her mouth, chasing it down with a glass of water in the hope it would soon sooth her headache.

After her brothers had started school Grace continued to travel into the city with her mother. Her Aunt Vivienne had since returned from Papua New Guinea, and now lived with her family south of the city centre. Sarah and Grace would ride the tram from the city to Salisbury to visit Vivienne, and Grace treasured those outings with her mother.

From the back steps Grace watched the workmen as they lay down sewerage piping into the long trench that had been dug along the back fence of the four houses in their street. After the piping was laid in the backyard, there was no need for the outhouse.

Her father and a friend extended the landing off the kitchen and built a small room at the end where they installed a ceramic toilet unit. What a luxury it was that they didn't have to go all the way down the back steps into the backyard to the outhouse.

Grace was relieved that the sawdust man would no longer be coming into their backyard to replace the outhouse waste bucket. She would wake up feeling very scared to the noise he made early each morning, thinking someone was climbing in her window. Every night, after she and her brother had gone to bed, Grace would tippy toe out to the lounge room and sit on her father's lap, as he watched television, until she fell to sleep. She felt safe in her father's arms. Safe from the nightmares she had from the strange noises in the night.

Now that Grace was going to school, Sarah insisted that Jack stop cutting her hair. Instead, she plaited Grace's hair in tiny plaits. As her hair grew longer, so did her plaits. Jack continued to cut the boys hair into a bowl cut because he could not afford the children to go to a hairdresser. He had his own mother cut his hair, and Jack paid for Sarah to go to a hairdresser so she could feel pampered.

Grace walked to school with her brothers which was just down the road from their house. When they arrived home in the afternoon, they usually found their mother sitting on the couch watching her favourite soap opera on their black and white television. As summer came to a close and autumn began, they were surprised one afternoon to find her up and about in the kitchen cooking and singing her favourite hymns.

'Hi, Mum!' they greeted.

'Hi, kids,' Sarah replied. 'Did you have a good day?'

'Yes.'

Grace and her brothers sat at the table, and Sarah placed a cup of chocolate milk and a freshly baked biscuit in front of each of them.

'How about after you're finished, you kids run down and pick me some mulberries so I can make a pie for dessert?'

'Yeah!' they squealed with excitement.

'Can you make custard as well please, Mum?' Grace added.

'Yes, certainly,' Sarah beamed.

When the children had finished their snack, they hurried down to the mulberry bush by the back fence. They kept every second berry for themselves, returning to the house with purple juice smeared across their faces.

'Oh dear,' Sarah laughed. 'Go wash your faces and hands before you touch anything.'

The berries simmered away in a shallow saucepan of water as Sarah made the custard in a pot. That night, she served up the hot mulberry pie for dessert. Paul used his spoon to vigorously swish the dark colour of the berries through the custard and ice cream. Grace preferred to slowly stir her spoon around, creating pretty purple swirls throughout the custard.

After the dishes had been washed, Grace and her brothers watched television with Jack in the living room until their bedtime. Sarah normally sat in the lounge with them knitting, but she was cooking. After the children had gone to bed, Jack approached the kitchen doorway, observing Sarah still hard at work.

'You've got lots of energy tonight.' Jack had never seen her so energized at night since her nursing days.

'I'm going to sleep now, Sarah.' She seemed totally engrossed in what she was doing and didn't respond.

Jack lay awake listened to Sarah making lots of noise in the kitchen. Finally it stopped, and the house was silent. Jack waited a few minutes to hear Sarah's footsteps coming down the hallway. He leaned over and switched on the lamp, sitting up on the edge of the bed. He stood to his feet and walked down the hall to the kitchen, but Sarah was not there.

The back door was still locked, so he reasoned that she wasn't in the toilet on the landing. He went into the living room and saw the front door slightly open.

Stepping out onto the porch he scanned the front yard, and then approached the footpath and looked both ways up and down the road. A cold breeze blew through the night, and there were no cars driving by at that late hour.

'Sarah!' Jack shone his torch into the dark and gloomy bush land next to the house. 'Sarah!'

He started walking along the side of the road, turning around when he reached the corner store and extending his search in the other direction. He crossed the road and walked around the block, but still he couldn't find her. It was no use, he thought. He could never find her on his own. He decided to return to the house in case Sarah had returned there.

Back at the house Jack phoned the police. Panicked and helpless, he sunk down in his armchair and waited. What if she was hurt, he thought. What if the police didn't find her? What if she ran into foul play? How far had she gone? He paced the floor, sat down, stood up, and paced some more.

'Why didn't she tell me where she was going?' he wondered.

The time on the clock next to the television ticked over into the morning. In the early hours, the phone rang. Jack jumped from the chair to pick up the receiver.

'Hello?'

'Jack, its Phillip.'

'Phillip?'

'Sarah is here, Jack. She's here at our house.'

Jack tensed his brows, shook his head.

'She's at your house?'

'Yes.'

He exhaled heavily, rubbing his forehead.

'I've been walking all over the neighbourhood looking for her. I called the police.'

'Well, she's safe here,' Phillip assured. 'She is very agitated though. She can rest here tonight, and we'll bring her home tomorrow afternoon.'

'Alright.' Jack sighed. 'Thank-you. I'm so sorry about this. I'm so glad she's okay.'

He hung up the phone.

'What's going on?' he thought to himself.

After calling the police, he collapsed into bed, the adrenaline draining from his body into the mattress. He was utterly exhausted, but his thoughts continued to tick over in his mind, stopping him from falling asleep. What would make her just walk out, he wondered. Why would she go to her parents' place?

Phillip and Aileen were at the house with Sarah, when Grace and her brothers arrived home from school. Her mother had dark circles under her eyes, her skin pale and washed out.

'Mummy is very tired, Grace,' said Aileen. 'She needs ter lie down.'

Phillip and Aileen helped Sarah into the bedroom, and then Aileen checked on Paul and Ryan playing in the backyard. Phillip pulled Grace aside, placing his hand on her shoulder as he knelt down in front of her.

'Now, you listen to me, sweetheart. Don't you go near your father, okay?'

'Why not?' Grace asked.

'He's been doing some bad things to your mother. You need to stay away from him. Now, go play with your brothers.'

Jack arrived home a short time later, and Phillip met him at the garage as he stepped out of the Austin.

'How is Sarah?' Jack enquired.

'She's sleeping,' Phillip replied.

'I was terrified for her,' Jack continued. 'I don't know why she'd do something like that. Did she say anything to you?'

'Yes, she did. Jack, I need to speak with you in private. Let's go inside.' Jack and Phillip sat at the kitchen table.

'Sarah was very distressed when she arrived at our house last night,' Phillip paused. 'She told us that you had hit her.'

'What?'

'Is it true, Jack? If it is, you're in a lot of trouble, you understand?'

'Phillip, I would never do such a thing! Never! You know me, I would never even think of doing something like that!'

Phillip said nothing.

'Come on, Phillip! Please believe me!' Jack begged, laying his hands open. 'Please! I would never hurt Sarah! I don't know why she would tell you that!'

When Phillip and Aileen left, Jack went into the bedroom and shook Sarah gently awake. She rolled over to look up at him through sleepy eyes.

'What is it, Jack?' She groaned.

'Did you tell your parents that I hit you?'

'What are you talking about?'

'Did you tell your father that I hit you?' Jack firmly persisted.

'No, Jack, I didn't!' Sarah insisted.

'Well then why did he tell me you did? He wouldn't lie! He wouldn't make it up!'

'I don't know why!' Sarah cried.

'Sarah, he thinks I'm some sort of monster!' Jack sighed, shaking his head. 'Have you said this to anyone else?'

'Jack, I don't remember saying anything like that! All I can remember is waking up at my parents' house this morning!'

Jack sat back, confused. Was she lying, or telling the truth? Could she have told anybody else? If she had, how many people now thought he was abusing her? And most of all, how could she not remember the previous night at all?

Chapter Nineteen

The house at Redcliffe was home for the Brooker family throughout the school holidays. At Christmas, Jack helped the children prop one of his painting planks against the window frame, creating a bridge that led down to the ground outside.

'Now Santa can come in and bring us our presents.' Grace said with excitement.

Jack drove the kids to the supermarket at the Redcliffe esplanade and gave each of them two dollars to buy presents for the family. Grace picked out a leaf-shaped bowl from the shelf; her mother could use it for the nuts she always put out to eat on Christmas day.

As Grace continued her hunt for presents, she spotted Ryan up ahead. Once they had found gifts for each other, the kids reconvened together in the back of the store, conspiring as to what they would buy for their father. Paul decided on a packet of handkerchiefs, and Grace and Ryan on tea mugs.

On Christmas Eve, Jack and the kids checked on the painting plank against the kitchen window, ensuring it was positioned correctly, so Santa wouldn't hurt himself on his way inside.

Their cousins Deborah, Tim and Ruth often stayed with them on holidays. They spent Christmas Day with their own families, and then by midday on Boxing Day, the Redcliffe house was filled with the chatter and activity of extended family. After a huge lunch, the men settled in front of the television to watch the cricket test between Australia and England. The kids played outside, while the women chatted over cups of tea on the porch.

Deborah, Tim and Ruth stayed on while their parents returned home to Brisbane. Jack had three weeks off over Christmas, and then returned to work in Brisbane, commuting back to the holiday house each evening. After breakfast each day, the children ventured outside to play.

Heavy on her feet, Sarah shuffled into the bedroom and closed the door. She sat down on the edge of the bed, brushing her hands over her face. Her migraine had set in. She reached over to the bedside table and popped two painkillers out of their packaging, swallowing them with a glass of water. She lay down and closed her eyes, quickly falling back to sleep.

It was low tide, and the kids played on the beach in front of the house.

'Let's build sand cities,' Ryan suggested.

He set to work constructing cardboard reinforced bridges, and each child attempted to build their houses more elaborate than the others. Making loud revving noises, Paul pushed his matchbox car around the sandy structures. Grace picked up another of his cars and chased him, making whirring sounds.

'I'm the police, Paul!' she shouted. 'Stop speeding right now!'

'Catch me if you can!' laughed Paul.

Sheavy the corgi puppy was a recent addition to the Brooker family. He planted himself in a watchful position in front of the sand city, and Grace charged him with protecting the city from intruders while they went into the house for lunch. Sheavy barked at a couple walking along nearby, settling when he sensed they were friendly. He stood up and trotted over to them, and the couple scratched him behind the ears. He didn't have a tail, only a stump, so his whole body waggled instead. All the kids came running out and giggled at the sight.

During the day the kids often returned to the house, running noisily through the living room to the kitchen for a drink. Grace paused for a moment by her parents' bedroom, approaching the closed door and pressing her ear against it.

She often heard, but never saw, her mother crying. Lately, she was always quiet in front of the children. Grace hated the sound of her mother's tears. What was making her so upset? Why did she cry all the time?

'Grace, come on!' Paul shouted.

She ran outside with the gang, and within minutes they were off on another adventure along the beachfront.

Their skin was brown from days of adventures in the sun. Their legs were long and lanky, and covered in bruises from climbing trees, jumping off walls and running around the yard.

One Christmas morning, Grace and her brothers squealed in delight at the new bicycles waiting for them at the foot of their beds. Paul and Ryan had new dragster bikes, while Grace had a regular blue bike with a basket and ribbons dangling from the handlebars. She was determined to keep up with her older brothers, be it at bike riding, fishing, swimming, football, or billy-cart racing. Whatever it was, she was insistent that she could do it too.

The holidays came to an end once again, and the family returned home to Keperra. Sarah decided to take the children to the nearby picture theatre at Gaythorne to see A Boy Named Charlie Brown. Jack strongly disapproved, claiming that the theatre was 'evil'. But Vivienne had taken her own children to see the film and had assured Sarah that it was nothing but an innocent cartoon.

At the front of the theatre, the seats were made of two wooden planks: one was positioned higher than the other, and between them hung hessian cloth. They were there for the children, and toward the back of the theatre there were regular chairs with firm, leather cushioning. The kids ran straight to the front and settled in with their ice cream and popcorn.

By 1971, Jack felt that the kids had outgrown the Redcliffe holiday house and decided to put the property up for sale. He bought another house on the Pumicestone Passage, further north along the Moreton Bay Peninsula.

***

The new place was a modern two-bedroom house supplied by rainwater tanks. The nearby bush land and the mangrove trees on the beach just down the end of the street was a breeding ground for mosquitoes and toads, which found their way into the house. The toilet room was sheltered under the roofline outside the back door, and Grace dreaded toilet runs in the middle of the night. The door was hinged four centimetres short of the floor, and each visit required a thorough search of every corner and under the toilet seat for spiders and toads. When she was satisfied there were none, she warily sat down on the seat, mosquitoes buzzing around biting at her bare flesh.

Shortly after purchasing the new house, Jack bought a Cruise Craft boat, and the children received water-skis that Christmas. They launched the boat from the ramp onto the Pumicestone Passage and motored over to nearby Bribie Island to the designated ski area.

Grace, Paul and Ryan and their cousins took it in turns skiing, while one sat in the boat with Jack and the others waited on the beach. Sheavy the dog would run along the strip of sand, and as the boat approached the shore, he paddled vigorously with his short legs all the way out into the water, barking over the wash as it splashed across his face. Within seconds the skier was gone, speeding away out into the depths again, and Sheavy turned around and paddled back toward the beach.

The neighbourhood was made up of seven unsealed streets: Third, Fourth, and Fifth Avenues all dirt roads. They were too rough for their go-carts, so Jack bought them two small motorbikes, which they raced up the roads and around in the surrounding bushland. The township was completely flat, and there was very little traffic down their end of the township. They spent their days riding their bikes, swimming, fishing, or walking up to the beach or the corner store.

***

During the holidays Jack had always driven back to the house in Redcliffe after work each day, as it was only a half an hour drive from Brisbane. He continued to do this for a short time after they had bought the new house, but another hour had been added to his commute, and he quickly grew weary of traveling the extra distance every morning and afternoon.

'I think I'm going to stay home in Keperra tomorrow night,' he stated to Sarah at dinner on Sunday night.

'Why?' asked Sarah.

'We're just that little bit further here from Brisbane than we were at Redcliffe. It's so much travel in one day. The kids are old enough to look after themselves most of the time, anyway. I'll come back up on Friday afternoon.'

Dusk had just fallen on Monday evening as Paul walked quickly down the street to the telephone box for their daily call to their father. He stepped inside and picked up the receiver, slipping a few coins into the slot. He dialled the number.

'Hello?'

'Dad, its Paul.'

'G'day. What did you get up to today son?'

'Mum is acting really weird, Dad. We're really scared of her.'

'What do you mean, acting strangely?'

'She was in bed all day, and now she's in the kitchen and talking really angry to herself. It's like she's possessed or something. We don't want to go near her. She's crazy, Dad.'

'Alright, Paul, I'll come up there straight away. You go back to the house and look after the others. I'll be there in about forty minutes.'

'Please hurry, Dad. We don't know what to do.'

'Don't worry, Paul, I'll be there very soon.'

The children met Jack as he pulled into the garage. They had been hiding in the yard. Jack could hear the noisy commotion in the kitchen. There, he found Sarah shuffling around, tossing pots and pans into the sink as she mumbled loudly to herself.

'Sarah?'

She looked at him briefly; her face was pale, and her eyes were puffy and bloodshot. Jack stepped forward.

'Paul called me and said you weren't well. Why don't you come and sit down for a little while?'

'I'm cooking dinner!' Sarah snapped. 'I'm busy!'

'Sarah, don't worry about dinner, its fine.'

Jack slipped his hand around her arm.

'Come on, Sarah,' he gently insisted. 'Why don't you come and lie down? I'll make something for dinner and tidy up the kitchen. Don't worry.'

Jack knew that if he could just get Sarah to bed, she would fall straight to sleep. He helped her lie down, and within minutes, she was asleep. Sitting by her side, he watched her in the dim light of the lamp. Another hospital visit was imminent.

'Dad, why does Mum act that way?' Grace asked as Jack returned to the living room.

Jack sighed, placing his hand on her shoulder.

'It's not your fault, sweetheart. I've never left you kids alone up here with her before; she's feeling stressed and anxious.'

The lights had just been turned out and everyone was drifting off to sleep, when suddenly an almighty thwack sounded from Paul's bed. Grace and Ryan sat bolt upright.

'What was that, Paul?' Grace hissed.

'An elephant beetle landed on the end of my bed. I kicked it from under the sheet.'

'Where did it go?' Grace asked, frantically searching her own bed.

'I don't know,' Paul replied. 'I hope it went back out the window!'

Grace wished her father would put mesh screens on the windows, like her cousins' houses had, to keep the bugs outside.

She often lay awake listening to the mosquitoes buzzing around her head, knowing they were looking for flesh to suck blood out of.

The next morning as Sarah slept, Jack prepared to drive back to Brisbane.

'I'll be back this afternoon, Paul,' he explained.

Paul nodded confidently.

'We'll be okay, Dad. We'll go down to the beach and the park and keep away from Mum.'

Late in the afternoon, Paul, Ryan, and Grace climbed up onto the roof of the house, where they could see out over the neighbourhood.

'Mum won't be able to find us up here.' Paul said, assuming leadership.'

That night, as she lay in bed, Grace closed her eyes and pressed the palms of her hands together.

'Dear God,' she whispered. 'Please help my family. I don't understand why Mum is sick all the time. I know it's hard for Dad to look after her, and there's no-one else helping us. I wish I could do more.'

There in the dark, Grace made a decision.

I am going to make Mum happy. I'll be happy and cheer her up. I'll help Dad and be really good and helpful.

Chapter Twenty

The tables in the church courtyard were covered with the usual spread of homemade cakes and biscuits. Grace chatted to her cousins Ruth and Deborah; they were all fifteen now, and she enjoyed spending time with them on Sundays. Nearby, a group of women talked amongst themselves.

'Did you see Sarah Brooker?'

'Goodness me, she's looking terrible these days!'

'She has gained so much weight over the years.'

'How could she still be suffering from ongoing grief from the loss of Daniel?'

'I don't know why she can't just pull her socks up and move on with her life. It's been thirteen years, for goodness sake!'

Grace felt her cheeks burn hot, with embarrassed at first, and then anger.

'They're supposed to be Mum's friends,' she thought. *'How could they talk about her like that?'*

At twelve years of age, Grace was starting to realise that their family was different in some ways to other families.

The sun was peaking over the horizon as Grace joined her brothers at the kitchen table. Her father was standing at the stove making porridge. Her mother shuffled in to sit at the kitchen table; her skin looked washed out, and she had dark circles under her puffy eyes. She was frightful to look upon and struggled to stay awake throughout breakfast. After Jack had left, she lifted her heavy frame from the chair and shuffled back to her bedroom. Grace hated the look of her mother. She was so scary and ugly.

Grace, Paul, and Ryan made their lunches. A few hours later when it was time to leave for school, they poked their heads into the main bedroom.

'Bye, Mum,' they called softly.

There was no reply.

As they walked down the hill towards their high school, Grace didn't join in on the boy's conversation, lost in her own thoughts.

'Why doesn't Mum ever want to get up in the morning and spend time with my brothers and me? Why doesn't she at least get up to say goodbye to us?'

Grace often walked home during her lunch break to check on her mother. She was usually in bed asleep but would wake up when she heard Grace call to her, and they would eat lunch together. Grace stepped into the house, crossed the living room and followed the hallway down to her parents' bedroom.

'Mum?' She pushed the door open a little further. 'Mum!'

She rushed into the room and dropped to her knees beside her mother, who lay slumped on the floor beside the bed.

'Mum! Mum! Wake up!'

Sarah didn't budge.

'What do I do, what do I do?' Grace panicked. 'Somebody help me! Please help me!'

Grace watched on as her mother was pushed on a wheeled stretcher out through the front door. A paramedic approached her.

'Do you know what medication she is taking?' he asked.

'Valium. And painkillers,' said Grace, wiping a tear away.

The paramedic placed his hand on her shoulder.

'We'll take care of your Mum now. Who can we contact to let them know what's happened?'

'You can call my Grandma.'

She gave him the number and he made the call from the home phone.

'Will you be okay?' he asked.

'Yes,' Grace quietly replied.

From the front door she watched the ambulance pull out onto the road and speed away, sirens ablaze. The house was still again. She walked into the kitchen and approached the sink, and with trembling hands filled a glass with water. She lifted it to her lips, swallowing the water one slow mouthful at a time.

Her legs were weak underneath her as she walked down the hill back to high school. As she approached the grounds, she heard the bell ring and quickened her pace. The lesson had already begun when she arrived at her classroom. The teacher narrowed her eyes at her as she stood nervously in the doorway.

'Grace, you're late,' she stated.

'I'm sorry, Miss.'

'Hurry up and take your seat.'

Grace hurried across the room and sat down at an empty desk. The teacher's words blurred as her mind lapsed back over the events of the past hour. She told no one what had happened.

When Jack arrived home in the afternoon, Grace and her brothers met him at the back door.

'Dad, Mum had to go to hospital,' said Grace.

'I know. The hospital rang Grandma Dot.' Jack placed his hand on his daughter's shoulder. 'Grace, I am so sorry that you had to see that.'

'Dad, is Mum alright?' Ryan asked.

'How do they fix that?' Paul asked. 'When someone takes too many pills?'

'They pump the person's stomach,' Jack flatly replied. 'She's alright now. They're looking after her.'

Grace stepped forward, peering at her father. 'Are you okay, Dad?'

Jack sighed deeply, shaking his head.

'I am so sorry, Grace,' he whispered. 'I really am.'

Grace nodded.

'I've got the vegetables ready to cook for dinner. They should be ready in about twenty minutes.'

'Thank you, sweetheart.'

No one was speaking at the table. Questions loomed like a thick dark cloud, but no knew how to start asking them.

'Dad?' Everyone looked to Grace. 'Did Mum take all those pills on purpose?'

Jack tensed his eyebrows, shaking his head.

'No, Grace.'

'I bet she did,' Paul scowled.

'Quiet, Paul!' Jack snapped. 'What an awful thing to say! Your mother is a good woman, and she wouldn't do something like that!'

Paul glared at his father. Jack reached over and took Grace's hand.

'She was just confused with her medication and took too much by accident.' He paused, looking thoughtfully at Paul and Ryan. 'She loves you all. She really does. She's just not well at all at the moment.'

'She never is,' Paul grumbled.

'That's enough!' Jack scolded. 'Now finish your meal! I don't want to hear another word!'

After the table was cleared and the dishes washed, Jack and the children sat down to watch television before bed. Jack stared blankly at the screen, letting the colours and noises absorb the chaos he was a part of.

At lunchtime the next day, Grace sat in the schoolyard with her friends.

'Hey Grace, why was your mum taken away in an ambulance yesterday?'

Grace froze.

'What?' She stammered.

'My mum saw it. And a few people have been talking about it around school. What happened?'

Grace hesitated, hastily concocting an answer.

'She fell down some steps. That's why the ambulance took her away.'

'Oh, okay.'

Grace remained quiet, munching away on her sandwiches as the other girls continued their conversation. It was only now that she was beginning to realize the full extent of her mother's illness.

The last few years had been a yoyo of her mother getting sick and well, sick and well, over and over throughout each year.

'Will it ever stop.' Grace thought.

The day after Sarah returned home from hospital, Jack arrived home from work and set his keys down on the kitchen table. He peered curiously down the hallway; there was noise coming from the bathroom, and there he found Sarah rummaging through the cabinets.

'Sarah, what are you doing?'

'I'm looking for my painkillers! I can't find them!'

'I've taken them away.'

Sarah stopped and glared at her husband.

'What! Why? Jack, I need them! Why are you doing this, Jack?'

'You're getting confused with your dosage and taking far too much. You almost killed yourself a week ago by taking too much, Sarah. Grace came home and found you on the floor. You could have died; don't you realize that?'

'Jack, you don't understand how much pain I'm in each day! I need them!'

'I know what your proper dosage is each day. I was there when the doctor prescribed them. I'll give you exactly the right amount in the morning, and then again at dinnertime.' Jack paused. 'You scared us, Sarah. Who knows what could have happened if Grace had not come home at lunchtime?'

'Jack, that is not fair! You don't understand!'

'Enough, Sarah. That is how it is going to be.'

Sarah pushed past Jack and stormed into the bedroom, slamming the door behind her.

Each day, Sarah searched every nook and cranny of the house for her pills. She found them every time, and Jack would have to find a new hiding spot for them. He knew that she despised him, but he stayed firm. One day Paul came storming out of the bedroom he shared with Ryan.

'Mum has been in our room!'

Jack sighed.

'I'm sorry, Paul.'

'She does it every day! She goes in there and moves our stuff around when she's looking for her pills!'

'I'll think of something, Paul. Don't worry.'

The next morning, downstairs in his work area underneath the house, Jack unlocked the heavy steel safe and took out the pill packets and bottles.

'Has our marriage come to this,' he wondered. *'Where did my bright intelligent wife go?'*

Sitting at the kitchen table, Sarah watched impatiently on the edge of her seat, her fists clenched as Jack unscrewed the lid of the Valium bottle and popped two painkillers out of their seal. He placed them in front of her, and Sarah swallowed them with a glass of water.

'Can I have two painkillers for later today, please?' she asked softly. 'I'll need them. Please, Jack?'

'Alright,' Jack sighed. 'Just two.'

Chapter Twenty-One

February slipped into March, and as the seasons changed from summer to autumn, so did Sarah's behaviour. With the cool weather setting in, she started baking instead of watching television. One day when Grace and her brothers arrived home from school in the afternoon, their mother had the glasses lined up on the bench ready for their malt milk and kept busy around the kitchen as they ate their snack. She briefly left the room, and Grace leant over to Paul.

'Mum's very energetic today!' she smiled.

'I know,' Paul frowned.

'She must be feeling better,' Grace continued.

'I am so happy to see her up and out of bed.'

Sarah cleaned the house all afternoon, barely noticing Jack when he arrived home at four o'clock.

'Your mum's very bright today,' Jack commented to Grace. 'Has she been like this all afternoon?'

'Yes,' Grace smiled.

'She's been singing and housecleaning and cooking.'

Grace was so relieved to see her mother so lively. Finally, her prayers had been answered, and she had a normal mother again. Maybe she could start inviting her friends over. It won't be so embarrassing anymore.

As the weeks passed, Sarah's behaviour continued to alter. After dinner and dessert, Sarah cleaned up the dishes, and kept busy around the kitchen long after the children had gone to bed. Jack wondered if she was angry with him, perhaps over the medication again. He went to bed alone, but the time passed, and she still didn't settle.

'*Not again,*' he thought.

He got up out of bed and found Sarah still fussing around the kitchen, doing nothing productive.

'Sarah, you're making a lot of noise. We're trying to sleep; the kids have got school in the morning, and I've got work.'

Sarah didn't stop, didn't look his way. Her speech was slurred as she mumbled to herself, her breathing heavy, and she shuffled her feet as she walked toward him.

'Get out of my way!' she snapped.

'Sarah!' Jack exclaimed. 'Listen to me! There's too much noise! It's late! It's time to settle down for the night!'

Jack sighed deeply, shaking his head as he turned and went back down the hall.

'*Here we go again*,' he thought tired and weary of the repetitive routine.

Lying in her bed with the light out, Grace had the blanket pulled up to her chin, her eyes fixed on the closed door. She was always scared at night, anxious that her mother would come in. She looked like a monster with her great big overweight body, bulging red eyes and messy hair. She would forget to shower for days, and she stank of perspiration.

Where had her quiet, gentle mother gone, Grace wondered. It was like she had turned into someone else. Why couldn't her father control her? How long would it go on for?

And to think she had been convinced that her mother was finally better.

Grace heard her parents' bedroom door open again, and her father's footsteps down the hall. She heard his voice in the kitchen.

'Sarah, let's go for a drive,' he suggested.

Jack led her by the arm down to the car.

Jack drove to the city hospital and took Sarah to the general admissions reception in the psychiatric ward. He was going to find out once and for all what was causing her to act in this bizarre way. Sarah sat quietly as they waited to be seen.

'Jack Brooker?' The man approached with his hand extended and shook Jack's hand. 'I'm Doctor Allen.'

Jack took Sarah's hand and they followed Dr. Allen to his office.

'Now, the nurse informed me that you're having a difficult time coping with Sarah at home?'

'Yes,' Jack replied. 'She's acting very strange. Her behaviour has changed very quickly in the past few weeks. She spends most of the day sleeping, but she's up until all hours of the night cooking and cleaning. She doesn't stop until three o'clock in the morning. I try to get her to come to bed, but she won't listen to me. It's as if she's in her own world and can't even hear me. This is not the first time this has happened, Doctor.'

Dr. Allen nodded.

'Is she on medication?'

'Valium and painkillers.'

Dr. Allen looked at Sarah, who sat quietly beside her husband.

'Have you been taking your medications correctly, Sarah?'

'Yes, Doctor. Jack has taken control of them and gives them to me every day.'

'She overdosed a fortnight ago,' Jack added. 'She was getting muddled with her dosage and had to go to hospital.'

Dr. Allen nodded.

'Alright, Sarah, I'm going to give you a general check-up now.'

Doctor Allen took Sarah's temperature and checked her heart rate and blood pressure. All the while, Sarah remained calm and quiet.

'Well, your blood pressure is higher than normal,' Dr. Allen stated. 'But aside from that, everything seems to be fine.'

'But it's not fine Doctor,' Jack insisted. 'She's not normally like this. What if we get home and she goes back to the way she was before we came here?'

'If that happens, bring her in again,' Dr. Allen insisted. 'I can't see anything wrong at the moment, so I'm afraid I can't admit her. Just continue to ensure she takes her medication correctly.'

Jack sighed, slumping back in his seat.

'I'm so tired, Doc. I've got to get some sleep.'

Sarah said nothing. Doctor Allen pulled his prescription pad in front of him.

'Sarah, I'm going to prescribe you with some sleeping pills,' he explained as he scribbled on the pad. 'They're only a small dosage but will help you settle down at night.'

He tore off the piece of paper and handed it to Jack.

'Now, I want you to stop doing so much housework, alright Sarah? Get some rest.'

Jack wondered what the hospital staff thought of him after their continuous visits. That he was a liar, that he was abusive toward Sarah. That he just wanted to get his wife out of the way. Maybe the doctor was right this time, he thought. Maybe she would calm down and things would go back to normal.

When they arrived home, Sarah took her pill and fell to sleep. In the morning, she joined the rest of the family for breakfast in her unsightly state. When Jack left for work, she went straight back to bed. Grace also went back to her bedroom, picking up her guitar. She practiced for a few hours each morning until it was time to go to high school. Just before she left with her brothers, she peered into her parents' bedroom.

'Goodbye Mum.' Silence followed.

That evening, Grace watched her mother as she attempted to make the evening meal. Mumbling and shaking her head, she looked so confused; her thoughts were so jumbled she could barely manage to make dinner anymore.

Once upon a time she had been an accomplished pianist and had played to the children, but now she could hardly play one hymn on their piano.

Grace stood from her chair and approached her mother.

'Can I help?' she asked.

Her mother grunted something indecipherable, and Grace left

her alone, retreating to her bedroom to practice her guitar.

That night as Sarah clambered around in the kitchen Jack lay awake in bed listening to the noise. It went on and on late into the night, and then the house fell silent. It was midnight when Jack picked up the telephone and dialled the police.

'Hello, my name is Jack Brooker. My wife Sarah is missing. She is not well; she is not thinking clearly. She has a mental condition and is under psychiatric care.'

Sitting in his armchair, Jack watched the clock as he waited for the phone to ring, for the knock on the door, for any news at all. He was now over tired and could only doze off for a minute here and there. He should have been used to this by now; Sarah was always found safe, but the possibility of the worse-case scenario always played on his mind.

'Will this time be bad news?'

There was a knock on the door, and Jack sprang up out of his chair, relief overwhelming him at the sight of Sarah with two police officers on the porch.

'Your wife told us she was going to work. She was on her way to the bus stop.'

Jack sighed, nodding.

'Thank you so much, officers. I'll take it from here.'

Sarah's walkouts continued. Until the early hours of the morning she was up and about in the kitchen, and then the front door closed, and the house was silent again. Jack could not stop her no matter what measures he took. The front door could be opened without a key, and he had to leave the key in the back door so that the family could get out to the toilet on the landing.

Sometimes Sarah didn't get far, and the police found her only a few streets from the house. Other times she made it all the way to the hospital and Jack was left to wonder how she'd managed to get there. The doctors would admit her for the night, and Jack collected her the following day.

Jack frequently took Sarah to the psychiatric ward himself, hoping they would admit her and relieve him and the family of the chaos for just a little while. Each time, Sarah miraculously managed to compose herself, and the doctors would not admit her.

Jack didn't tell his friends at church the whole truth about Sarah's condition. It was too embarrassing. Even the doctors didn't believe him when he told them how she had been behaving.

After another tiring month, Jack drove Sarah back to the hospital. In the passenger seat, Sarah murmured to herself, fidgeting her hands. At the hospital, a team of doctors assessed Sarah for several hours before finally agreed to admit her.

Grace and her brothers were waiting for their father when he arrived back at the house. Each time he took their mother to the hospital, they hoped he would return without her. They saw the ute pull up outside and breathed a sigh of relief when they saw him get out of the car alone.

'At last, we can get some sleep,' thought Grace.

In Sarah's absence, peace was once again restored in the Brooker household. As he did every time Sarah was admitted to hospital, Jack re-organized the family's schedule, delegating chores to each of the kids to help with the daily running of the household. New information was coming through from the doctors, and he called a meeting with Sarah's parents to update them on her condition.

'The doctors are saying that Sarah has had a nervous breakdown,' Jack explained. 'That's why she's been acting so strangely.'

'What is a nervous breakdown?' asked Aileen.

'They said it's a psychological collapse,' Jack continued. 'It happens when a person experiences severe depression. Or after a long period of stress which has not been dealt with. It's worse than the doctors previously thought; because she wasn't treated correctly to begin with, her condition has worsened.' Jack sighed, scratching his forehead. 'I've been seeking help for her for years, and all the treatments and pills seem to have been for nothing.'

Jack paused, looking to Phillip.

'Phillip, do you remember when Sarah told you that I had hit her?'

'Yes,' Phillip replied.

'Well, she has these episodes of strange behaviour, and it makes her do and say things she normally wouldn't. She gets confused and is not herself. She doesn't remember the incidents either.'

Phillip nodded. 'I understand. So, it's been going on for that long?'

'Yes.'

Read Grace's Poem 'A Daughter's Trust' in Part 4

Chapter Twenty-Two

Dr. Buchanan was the latest in a long list of physicians tasked with caring for Sarah. By now, Jack was struggling to keep up with them all.

'Mr. Brooker, I have been working with other doctors here at the hospital in examining Sarah whilst she's been here with us. We believe we have a definitive diagnosis for her condition.'

Jack raised his eyebrows. 'Really?'

'Yes. Our tests and observations indicate that Sarah is suffering from a mental disorder known as Schizophrenia.'

Jack shrugged, shaking his head.

'What is that?'

'It is an illness that affects the normal functioning of the brain. It interferes with a person's ability to think, feel, and act. Some patients do recover completely, and with time most find that their symptoms improve. However, for many, it is a prolonged illness, which can involve years of distressing symptoms. If not receiving treatment, patients with Schizophrenia experience persistent symptoms of psychosis, like disordered thinking, delusions, and hallucinations. Other associated symptoms are low motivation and changed feelings.'

Doctor Buchanan glanced at his notes.

'I've prescribed Sarah with the appropriate medication, and I've referred her to a psychiatrist with whom she will have regular visits.'

***

Passing by the main bedroom, Grace spotted her mother sitting on the end of the bed, her Bible open on her lap. She looked up and smiled.

Grace sat down next to her mother.

'What are you reading Mum?'

'Oh, my favourite verses, listen…'

Grace sat there, stunned and silent, looking at her mother flicking through her Bible, reading verse after verse.

'How can she sit there so calm after tormenting us and herself for months with her crazy behaviour? Is she better for good this time, or will the monster in her reappear again soon?'

Grace never heard her mother voice disappointment or blame toward anyone, including God, for her illness.

Sarah was at her most peaceful at the holiday house. She still slept for most of the day, but when she was up out of bed, she seemed content. There was a small veranda off the kitchen under the shelter of the roof, and there she would knit while she watched the children kick the football around the yard. Life was calm again.

It was usually three months from the onset of a psychotic episode and when Sarah returned home from hospital. Between episodes Sarah suffered from depression and slept most of the time. Grace longed for her mother to be well enough to answer questions about her changing teenage body and help her with her homework. She struggled on trying to figure it all out by herself. She just managed to pass her year ten exams.

Aileen spoke to Sarah during the week on the phone, but rarely visited her at home in Keperra. Jack thought that it was because she didn't know how to handle Sarah's illness and suspected that perhaps her daughter embarrassed her. When the children were younger, Jack and Sarah had taken them to visit Aileen and Phillip for lunch on Sundays after church. Now that their mother's health had deteriorated, the children now teenagers, didn't see much of their grandparents anymore.

***

Resting his chin in his hand, Jack struggled to keep himself awake. The phone rang, and he jumped for it and answered it quickly, hoping it hadn't woken the children.

'Hello?'

'Jack, its Phillip. Sarah is here; she's with some strange man.'

Jack felt his stomach sink inside him.

'Who is he?'

'I don't know, Jack. He says his name is Kevin. Do you know anyone by that name?'

'No, I don't.'

'I didn't think so. He looks like a homeless person; I don't know where Sarah found him. She must have come across him somewhere between your house and ours. She was raving on about how much she loved him, and that she was going to marry him.'

Jack felt his heart sink.

'Where are they now?' he asked.

'I told this 'Kevin' fellow to leave, or we would call the police. We can keep Sarah here overnight and drop her home tomorrow.'

'Alright, thank-you, Philip. I'm sorry about all this.'

Jack hung up the phone and sank back down into his chair. Each night he spent hours gripped with fear as he awaited news about Sarah. The idea of her wandering deliriously through the dark night terrified him, and his worst fear was always that she would run into harm's way. Kevin was the only one he knew about, but how many others could there have been?

The following day, Jack took Sarah to the hospital, and she was admitted. After further observation, he was called to another meeting with Doctor Buchanan.

'I would like to transfer Sarah to a different hospital in Wacol, where she can receive Electroconvulsive Therapy.'

'What is that?' Jack queried.

'It is a psychiatric treatment,' Dr Buchanan explained. 'Patients are anesthetized, and seizures are electronically induced for therapeutic effect. It is used in cases of severe depression like Sarah's, where the patient has not responded to other treatments.

It will erase her memories.'

'Erase her memories? Why would you want to erase her memories?'

'The procedure will erase the ones that are causing her depression. Hopefully, this will help Sarah finally move on from her past traumas and lead a normal life again.'

Jack shook his head.

'I don't know how I feel about that. It sounds horrible.'

'It is the best treatment I can recommend for her at this stage.'

The kids had finished the washing up and the boys had retreated to their bedrooms. Ryan gently strummed away on his guitar, and Paul's battery-operated radio quietly played the Beatles Show. He listened to the program every night, on which the hosts played the band's rebellious music and discussed the cryptic messages the songs allegedly carried. Jack sat in the living room watching the television, and Grace sat down on the couch.

'Dad?'

'Yes, love?'

'I want to go and see Mum.'

Jack looked at his daughter.

'She's been in hospital for a few months now,' Grace went on. 'I miss her. Can we go and see her?'

'Grace, the hospital where she is now is not like the others. It is not a nice place to visit. It's very unpleasant, and there are a lot of very sick people there. I don't think you'll like being there at all.'

'I really want to see her,' Grace insisted.

'I can understand that you miss your mother dearly, Grace. I really can, but...'

'Please, Dad? Please take me?'

Jack sighed, rubbing his forehead. 'Let me think about it, okay?'

Grace left her father to watch television, and Jack pondered her request. She was fifteen years of age and had seen her mother sick many times before. She would probably be able to handle seeing Sarah in the hospital, but he would take her only once.

***

On Saturday morning Jack drove Grace to Wacol, southwest of Brisbane. He pulled into the parking lot outside the hospital building, and as Grace reached for the door handle, he stopped her.

'Wait,' Jack hesitated. 'Are you sure you want to do this?'

Grace nodded.

'Yes Dad. I'm sure.'

Inside the building, they approached the front desk, where there sat a nurse.

'Can I help you?'

'My name is Jack Brooker, and this is my daughter Grace. We're here to see Sarah Brooker.'

The nurse placed a clipboard on the desk in front of them.

'Sign in, please. Visiting hours finish at four.'

Walking through the stark white corridors of the old building, Grace observed residents dressed in pyjamas and bathrobes, staring at her with red puffy eyes and mumbling like her mother often did. Grace looked away, avoiding eye contact and she took her father's hand.

They arrived at a recreation room, where frail human bodies were slumped in wheelchairs, staring blankly at the television set. Jack opened the door, and Grace took a deep breath, stepping inside. There sat her mother slouched in a wheelchair by the window.

'Why don't you go over and say hello?' Jack suggested.

Grace hesitated, then took a few steps into the room. Her mother's face was drawn and weary, and there were deep dark circles under her eyes. Her hair, once upon a time lush brown and wavy, was now wiry with hints of grey.

'Mum?'

Grace reached down and placed her hand over her mother's. Her limp hand didn't move under Grace's warm touch.

'Mum? It's me, Mum. It's Grace.'

Sarah slowly turned her head, but didn't lift her eyes, her empty gaze lingering on the floor. Grace looked up at her father standing nearby.

'She doesn't recognize me, Dad.'

'She has been through some very intense treatment recently, sweetie.'

Grace shook her head.

'What sort of treatment is it?' she exclaimed. 'Look at her! I hate this place, Dad! I want to take Mum home with us!'

Jack took a step forward, holding his hands up, shaking his head.

'I'm sorry, but we can't do that, Grace. Mum has to stay here to get well again.'

'Get well from this? How will that ever happen?' Grace waved her finger at her mother. 'Dad, look at her! She's like a zombie! What have they done to her?'

'Grace, calm down,' Jack soothed, touching her tense shoulders. Sarah turned her empty gaze back to the window.

Read Grace's Poem 'Why Mummy?' in Part 4

Chapter Twenty-Three

Grace's Aunty Hilary, her mother's younger sister, lived with her husband and two children on the Gold Coast one hour south of Brisbane. For many years they had lived in a big waterfront house right on a canal, and now lived in a big house that they built on a large property in the hinterland. Grace loved visiting her aunty there; Hilary was always so gentle and kind, a light amidst the dark and melancholy cloud that had hung over Grace's teenage years. Hilary never asked her much about life at home, and Grace was happy not to talk about it.

Hilary had invited Grace to come and stay with her and her family for a few weeks over the Christmas holidays. Sitting on the balcony, Grace looked out over the pond in front of the house. The magpies and other birds were busy flitting about in the surrounding gum trees. The screen door creaked, and Grace looked up to see Hilary step outside. She approached Grace, sitting down next to her. She was holding a book in her hands.

'I know you must have been through a very difficult time with your mother.'

Grace nodded solemnly.

'Yeah…it's pretty bad.'

Hilary gave the book to Grace.

'I'd like you to have this. It is a gift, just for you. It is about healing from life's difficulties. I hope you find it encouraging.'

Grace took the book, and Hilary hugged her niece, her embrace warm and comforting. She sat back and took Grace's hand, looking into her eyes.

'You're welcome to stay as long as you want to.'

'Thanks, but I've applied for a few jobs in Brisbane, and I'm hoping I'll get one of them in the New Year.'

Hilary smiled, squeezing Grace's hand.

Hilary stood, leaving Grace to enjoy the peaceful surrounds.

One day while Grace was walking down by the lake, Hilary called out to her.

'Grace, it's your dad on the phone.'

Grace ran up to the house and picked up the receiver.

'Hi, Dad.'

'Hi, Grace. I just had a phone call from the bank. You got the job; you start next week.'

'Ahhh!' Grace cried, jumping up and down in excitement.

At last, her own money. She would have to wait until she was eighteen to move out of home, but she would waste no time in doing so when the time arrived. She could make plans to move out, travel, whatever she wanted to do. Soon, she would have control of her life, away from her mother.

Read Grace's Poem 'A Mothers Hug' in Part 4

Chapter Twenty-Four

Upon opening her heavy eyes, Grace found her body to be in a state of sleepy resistance as she moved to get up. It seemed as if she had just been able to drift off when she had been jolted awake by her alarm clock. She did not want to move. She needed more time. She had laid awake until the early hours of the morning, only able to sleep when her mother's noisy antics had finally ceased. Facing the day seemed like an impossible feat.

The rhythmic swaying of the diesel train sent Grace into a fleeting doze, from which she was abruptly awoken when her head tipped sharply forward. She was exhausted and her workday had only just begun.

Grace had grown accustomed to functioning while sleep deprived but learning to cope had not made it any easier. It was still an uphill battle to make it through the day. She made it to her morning break, taking her bag and retreating to the restroom. She shut herself away in a cubicle, feeling the emotions surge forth with force, washing over her like a wave dumping her on the beach. She sunk down on the toilet seat, resting her elbows on her knees and dropping her head forward, smothering her quiet sobs with her hands.

'If only I could just take a nap.'

She hated living at home. Her mother's weird behaviour scared her.

'Why can't dad control mum? Why did he let her keep acting in this bizarre way?'

They all thought she would be better forever each time she came out of hospital, but the chaos would happen over and over, again and again.

The restroom door opened, and she froze where she sat, holding in her quiet sobs. She heard the toilet flush, footsteps, then the tap, footsteps and the door swinging open and closed. She breathed again, pulling toilet paper from the dispenser beside her to soak up the tears from her face. She took a deep breath, stood and paused, listening again. When she was sure she was alone, she opened the cubicle door and approached the mirror, looking at her reflection. Her face was flushed red from crying. She couldn't go back to her desk looking like this.

'You have to get it together before you go back out there,' she thought to herself as she brushed her hair. *'You have to cope and be strong. You can't talk to anyone about it, or they might think you're mentally sick too.'*

When the colour had returned to her face, Grace took another deep breath and returned to her desk.

Jack was sitting in the living room when Grace arrived home that evening. He switched off the television; it was as if he had been waiting for her. Her brothers were already home, and Jack called them together for a family meeting.

'The hospital rang today,' Jack began. 'Grandma Aileen has deteriorated.'

Grace looked across the table at her brothers.

'Maybe we shouldn't go on the trip.' She looked back at her father. 'What if she dies while we're away?'

Jack paused thoughtfully.

'No, you should go.' He looked up at Grace, and then at Paul and Ryan. 'You need the break. Go, and forget about life here for a while.'

With Ryan's blue Cortina station wagon packed up with camping gear, Grace and her brothers headed southbound for Melbourne. They had never been outside of Queensland; travelling along the East Coast of Australia, the lush green hills and mountains that rolled through New South Wales and Victoria were so different to the dry, parched Queensland landscape she had grown up with.

Once in Melbourne, they travelled south of the city centre to the Mornington Peninsula, a string of village communities curled around the south-eastern flank of Port Phillip Bay. They continued to travel east until they reached their final destination, Phillip Island.

The youth camp site was similar to the camp they had stayed at every year on the Gold Coast. A solid brick mess hall, with rows of cabins on either side. That evening, Grace sat with her hut leader and the other girls from her cabin as they waited to join the line to collect their dinner. A boy with long blonde hair and bronzed skin sat at a table across the way; he was very handsome, and she loved his aura of rebellion. He looked at Grace, and she quickly looked away, her cheeks flushed with embarrassment. His table was called upon to collect their dinner, and Grace dared to look up again, seeing him as he passed by her table. He was close enough now that she could see that his eyes were piercing blue.

'Hi,' he smiled.

'Hi,' Grace murmured, sheepishly averting her eyes again.

***

Rugged up in her beanie, scarf and jumper, Grace watched on from the beach as Alex surfed the cold grey waves. He wore a full-length wetsuit, and still Grace shuddered at the sight of him in the water. She was comfortable and warm in her new flared denim jeans. She felt rebellious in them; they were no ordinary garment, a symbol of her newfound free will. They were the first pair of pants she had ever owned. Women in her church were forbidden from wearing pants or makeup. They lived a life of many restrictions, and Grace had been astounded to discover that some of the other young people in her youth group didn't even have a television set in their home. Now that she was earning her own money, she would wear jeans and makeup everywhere except to church.

Alex came up the beach, dropping his surfboard on the sand.

He picked up his towel and dried off, sitting down next to her.

'I wish you didn't have to go home tomorrow.'

Grace smiled sadly at him.

'Will you write to me?'

'Of course. Every week. Make sure you write down your phone number for me too.'

Grace ignored her brothers' teasing as they travelled back up along the East Coast toward home. She was head over heels in love, and she didn't care what they thought of it. Gazing out the window, the breathtaking landscape passed by her eyes, but she didn't take it in. Her mind was elsewhere, replaying every precious moment of the last week over and over in her mind.

The first letter was waiting for Grace when she and her brothers arrived home. Stepping into her room, she spotted the letter lying on her bed. Dropping her bag on the floor, she snatched it up, tearing it open and pulling out the piece of paper. Sinking down on the edge of the bed, her smile spread across her face as she read. She pressed the letter to her chest, where butterflies flitted around her heart.

On Monday morning Grace floated back to work on cloud nine. With her reply letter to Alex sealed in an envelope, she approached the letterbox outside the inner-city post office. She opened the lid and dropped the envelope in, already anxious for Alex's reply. As she went through the mundane motions of her workday, he was never far from her mind. Her weeks revolved around anticipating the next letter, the next phone call. She let lovesickness consume her; it was all a welcome distraction from the routine chaos that continued to unfold at home. As Grace lay awake at night, her mother clamouring around the house, she escaped into her own thoughts, her memories of her time with Alex providing a time travel portal out of her current nightmare.

Read Grace's Poem 'Attraction' in Part 4

Chapter Twenty-Five

Instead of the youth camp that she usually attended with her brothers at Easter time, Grace had saved up $600 to fly to Melbourne to visit Alex. Instead of bathers and towels, she packed her bag with beanies, scarves, jumpers and jeans. On Thursday evening, Jack drove her to the airport. The flight to Melbourne via Sydney took just over four hours.

The Bells Beach Surf Classic competition was held annually at Easter time. Grace and Alex spent Good Friday attending his church's service, then spending the rest of the day with Alex's parents and friends from church. They had to wait until Saturday before they could make the hour and a half drive to watch the world's best surfers compete. They started the journey early in the morning, following the Great Ocean Road as it wound its way alongside the wild and windswept Southern Ocean.

Grace breathed in deep the freedom she felt. Alex oozed confidence, made her laugh and was exciting to be with. He opened up a whole new world of fun and adventure to her.

They arrived at Bells Beach to find a crowd of spectators already gathering, securing their vantage points along the cliffs. The high cliffs provided a dramatic backdrop to the natural amphitheatre of the beach and large ocean swells. The reef-strewn shallows created world class surf.

Alex lived with his parents in Montmorency, a suburb north-east of the city centre. His family belonged to the same strict religion as Grace's family, and Alex was under strict instructions from his parents to be back home before ten o'clock each night.

Once they finished church on Sunday, they drove back to Bell's Beach. Too soon the long weekend came to an end. The weather was grey and miserable on Easter Monday, the morning of Grace's flight home, the sun peeping through the clouds every now and then as Alex drove her to the airport. Grace reluctantly got out of his car, her heart heavy with lovesick longing as she said goodbye again.

***

The telephone rang in the living room, and Grace held her breath in anticipation as she waited. Her father called out to her, and she came bounding down the hallway.

The land line phone sat on a bench in the living room, right beside Jack's armchair where he sat to watch television in the evening. In the kitchen Sarah was preparing dinner, so Grace stood awkwardly in between, her voice lowered as she spoke to Alex.

'I have some news,' said Alex on the other end of the line. *'I'm moving to Brisbane!'*

'Oh wow, that's great!' Grace exclaimed. I can't wait!'

***

Grace's bag lay open on her bed as she packed toiletries, changes of clothes, bathers and a towel. She turned to see her father pass her bedroom. He paused for just a second, narrowing his eyes at the bag.

Grace had spent very little time at home over the past six months. Each Friday after work, Alex would pick her up in his blue Toyota Corolla station wagon, and they would drive down to the Gold Coast, with Larry Norman and Gerry Rafferty playing on the brand-new cassette car stereo. They followed the surf, going wherever the swell was big, be it Kirra, Surfers Paradise, Burleigh Heads or Duranbah Beach. Grace told her father she was staying with friends overnight, while she and Alex slept in the back of his Corolla wagon.

Kirra Beach wrapped around the bend which separated it from Coolangatta in front of Kirra Hill. Weatherboard beach shacks stood amongst the hotels, shops and cafes.

As Alex surfed, Grace was content to watch from the beach, the sun warm on her skin. She had immersed herself into his life; it was so much more exciting than her boring crazy life at home. A big, wide exciting world was opening up to her, and she was loving it.

In the afternoon they drove on to Duranbah Beach, the northernmost beach in New South Wales. Duranbah was situated between the mouth of the Tweed River and the rocky headland of Point Danger, which marked the Queensland and New South Wales state border.

Grace had no interest in learning how to surf, but she loved this 'surfie chick' lifestyle. She never tired of sitting on the beach while Alex surfed, savouring the peace and quiet and being a part of the surfside landscape. There, she was free to read, go for a walk along the beach, go for a swim or fall to sleep on her beach towel to the rhythmic sound of the ocean waves crashing on the shoreline.

One Saturday night outside Grace's house, Alex turned to face her, leaning over the centre console and kissing her softly. Grace's heart raced, partly with excitement, partly with nervousness. She kept her eyes open, watching the front door of the house. Alex gently pulled away, looking at her with his dreamy blue eyes.

'I had better go inside,' said Grace, reaching for the door handle.

'Grace…' Alex touched her arm. 'I need to tell you something.'

Grace sat back, turning her body back to face him.

'What is it?'

Alex sighed.

'I've had an offer for a great work opportunity back in Melbourne. I've decided to move back.'

'What? Why didn't you tell me over the weekend?'

'I didn't want to ruin the weekend.'

'Grace!' She looked out the window to see her father standing at the front door.

'I have to go.'

'I'll pick you up tomorrow morning for church.'

'Okay. We can talk then.'

Alex's Corolla was packed full of his belongings. Grace stood with him next to the driver's door, where they had been holding each other for several minutes.

'Make sure you write to me every week,' She whispered.

Alex nodded.

'I'll call you every week too.'

He let her go, opening the door and sliding into the driver's seat. He leaned out the window, and she kissed him once more. He pulled out onto the road, and she watched the wagon until it disappeared behind the blur of her tears.

After Alex's return to Melbourne, Grace's life continued as normal during the week, but her weekends were now gaping holes of emptiness. Even when she spent time with her friends, Grace still missed her life with Alex. Her spirits were lifted with every letter and phone call, but the blissful joy was fleeting.

At night, Grace tossed in the dark as she lay awake at night. The blissful reminiscing of memories on these disrupted nights had become desperate longings. Her eighteenth birthday was just months away. She would be an adult then, free to make her own choices. Her transition from adolescence to adulthood was her pathway to freedom, and she would not wait a moment longer than necessary to make her escape.

Read Grace's Poem 'First Date' and 'Budding Love' in Part 4

Chapter Twenty-Six

Sarah had been well for some time in the lead-up to Grace's departure, and on her daughter's eighteenth birthday she joined Jack and his parents as they accompanied Grace to the airport. There, Grace could not contain her excitement. She knew that her parents were trying to act happy for her, but she could see the sadness behind their smiles. She was the first child to leave home, and she wasn't moving somewhere else in Brisbane, but two states away. She could not wait to get away; she could see now that the crazy, emotional rollercoaster that she rode within their family home would never stop to let her off. So now she was taking herself off, swapping the rollercoaster for an airplane. Her boarding pass was her ticket to freedom.

'Are you ready?' said Jack.

'I think so,' Grace smiled.

'Remember, if you need anything, or you want to come back, just call. Any time of the day or night.'

Grace nodded; confident she wouldn't need to take him up on the offer. She would never go back to her crazy mother or any part of her old life. She hugged both of her parents and grandparents, smiling and waving back at them as she boarded the plane. Inside the aircraft, she followed the narrow aisle along to her seat. More and more people boarded, and as Grace watched the cabin fill up, in her mind's eye she could still see her parents' sad faces as she had so happily and boldly waved goodbye.

The plane began to move toward the runway. Grace felt the force push her body back into the seat. A pang of guilt seized her heart, flooding into her body and weighing heavily inside her, pulling her down into her seat like the gravity as they lifted off the runway. She was being a selfish teenager, she knew, but she was only trying to survive. As the plane climbed higher into the sky, Grace smiled to herself. She was destined for a new city, a new future. The rest of her life awaited her at the other end of this flight.

Read Grace's Poem 'Cliff Edge of Love' in Part 4

Part Four: Poems By Grace

The Wilted Rose Poetry

Written by Grace after the first edition of The Wilted Rose as she reflected back over her life.

1. My Baby Brother
2. A Daughter's Trust
3. Why Mummy?
4. A Mother's Hug
5. Attraction
6. First Date
7. Budding Love
8. Cliff Edge of Love
9. The Web of Love

My Baby Brother

Hello, my precious baby brother
I'm so angry, so upset
I woke too late, I missed the chance

To say goodbye that morning.
Dad and your two brothers
Stood on the back veranda
Looking up into the sky

Squinting in the morning sun.
I asked them curiously
'What are you all doing?'
As I found a space on the staircase

To look up at the empty sky.
'Watching Daniel go to heaven'
Is what my father said
'Why didn't you wake me up in time
So I could say goodbye?'

God wanted you to live with him
He stole you from my family
Not even considering
How hurt that would make us feel.

Our grandfather ruled
'No children at the funeral'
I once more was denied
The chance to say goodbye.

Mummy was crying in her bed
Bleeding from her broken heart
Confused and upset, it was tragic
Daddy broke down and cried.
Grandad told Daddy 'Stop crying Son,

Wipe your tears, be a man
You have responsibilities
Trust in God to meet your needs.

Sorrow filled the walls
Of our young family home
Desperate prayers floated up

To the selfish God who stole you from us.

Day followed night
And life barged on
With no regard
For the pain it did impart.

Daddy swallowed his tears
And went back to work
Mummy was left at home
With three kids in toe.

The seasons came and went
The sun burnt us with pain
The full moon left us cold
The rain drenched our souls.

Mummy's pain did not heal
Her tears drenched her bed
Doctors came, she took some pills
She couldn't mother her three kids.
So, she returned to hospital
Where they tried to 'make' her well
A pill will solve her problem
But who will care for the children?

Grandad forced Daddy
To put us in an orphanage
Family and friends won't help you, son

Her illness is too embarrassing.'

Orphaned by our mother
Orphaned by our father
Orphaned by the selfish God
Who stole away my brother.

'You can visit on Saturday'
Is what the matron told my dad
My brothers cried and begs him
To take us away from there.

Mummy came home sedated
Now she cries and sleeps a lot
Goes through the motions of daily living
Cooking, cleaning, weekly shopping.

I tugged on her dress to get her attention
'I missed you mummy; I miss Daniel still'
She sighed deeply and touched my face
With tears welling up in her eyes.

Her sorrow too deep for mere words
Her eyes and posture said it all
Life would never be the same
Mummy would never be happy again.
Where did my mum go when my brother died?
They took her away then sent her home
But they kept her smile, her heart, her soul
They killed her desire to love us all.

Is God sitting up in his peaceful 'heaven'
Delighting in the company of my brother
While down here we continue to suffer

While Daddy prays to that same God each day.
I was only three

My brothers four and five
Too young to understand

And no one thought to explain.
Now an adult, I know the truth
That God did not selfishly steal you
That you died suddenly in 1963
From a serious illness no one could fix.

A Daughter's Trust

Religious rules of black and white
Of should and shouldn't, right and wrong
You can, you can't, you must obey

God is watching how I behave.
Break the rules and you will perish
Be isolated and alone
From everyone you've ever loved
And burn in hell with the devil.

The innocent child
Looked up at her father
With trusting eyes
Obeying this order.

Not only her father
But her grandpa too
Taught her this belief
For her own safety.

'I trust you daddy
You're bigger than me
You're older and smarter
You'll look after me.'

'I will follow your rules
I will not disappoint
You can count on me
To obey perfectly.'

'I need you to look at me
With your approving smile
To say 'Well done my child
I'm pleased you won't perish.'

'Dad, you're my prince
My knight in shining armour
You're the type of man
I want to marry.'

Her father never got mad at her
Though he did toward her brothers
With disapproval in his eyes
She was sure they would perish.

She was always sweet
Obedient and kind
So, her father wouldn't frown
And look disappointed.

She needed her father
The sane adult in her life
To protect her from the scary one
The monster called 'Mummy'.

'Daddy, though my mum is sick
Absent most of the time
You feed me and cloth me
And protect me from harm.'

'I need your love
I need your care
For my very survival
To exist in this world.'
She was too young to understand
The difficult time her daddy faced
In the 1960s, it was not easy
Living with mum's mental illness.

Why Mummy?

Mum, why did you send me to the orphanage?
I got left there, cared by people unknown
I was so young. I needed your love?

Mum, why didn't you get out of bed
After my baby brother died
Wasn't I worthy of your time?
I was only 3, you forgot about me.

Mum, why did you throw the cup at me?
I was excited about going to kindy
I was only 5. Why be so unkind?

Mum, why didn't you join in my birthday party?
I looked for you, but my aunty said
You were not feeling well and resting in bed
I was only 6, you could have made an effort?

Mum, why did you make me iron the hankies
Knowing I'd burn my fingers trying
I was only 8, for goodness sake.

Mum, why did you take back the dress you bought me
And say to me 'It's mine, not yours?'
I was only 9, you stole what was mine.

Mum, why did you give to our dog
My favourite stuffed toy
Then watch him chew it up
I was only 12, you broke my heart.
Mum, why did you take the overdose
I thought you were dead, lying on the floor
I came home from school to have lunch with you

I was only 15, was I not worth living for?

Mum, why did you dose up my baby daughter
With pain medicine while I was at work
I had to leave my job to protect her from you
I needed your help, but I couldn't trust you.

Mum, why did you go back to bed
When I'd visit with your granddaughter?
We waited and hoped for your company
But we waited in vain. So, we stopped coming your way.

A Mother's Hug

The little girl stood still and quiet
At the bedroom door mid-morning
Looking anxiously into the dark room
Toward her mother's bed.

She could see her form under the sheets
'Is she asleep or just resting?'
She tippy toed into the room
And stood beside mother's bed.

Her mother's eyes were shut, her breathing soft
So she turned around and walked back out
'I'll try again latter when she's awake
I won't disturb mummy while she sleeps.'

The teenage girl stood at the bedroom door
'Mum I'm leaving for school now'
Waiting for her mother to rise out of bed
To give her a hug and say, 'I love you dear.'

The moment passed; silence stayed
'Is she awake or just ignoring me?'
In disappointment she turned and left
Her mother lay there in silence.

Treasured moments with her mother
Few and far between
A daughter longs and waits
For her mother's nurturing hug.

Attraction

We walked and talked
Laughed and smiled
We sat close, energy rose
We hugged and kissed.

The tone of his voice
Rumbled through my body
He's tall and handsome
He made me laugh.

I dived in boots and all,
I talked too much, shared my soul
Now I'm just feeling vulnerable.

Now it's awkward, uncomfortable
The truth is revealed, my fate is sealed
I bubble with nerves and excitement
Could he love someone such as this?

It's not so much could he love me
For I feel sure he could love me dear
It's more about can I love me
Well, I guess, only time will tell.

I must confess my question is
Could he love somebody like me?
More so, could I allow myself
To let love run away with me.

I started out feeling
Strong and in control
Now things look bleak,
I'm weak at the knees.

I'm magnetized by his attention
You're a willing, captive audience
Look at me, look at me
I dance, I sing, I write poetry.

I thought I'd ticked off the 'responsible' chart
But when I took the test I didn't pass.

I try hard to work, but I think of you
My passion looms in my thoughts of you
To be responsible, is proving impossible.

Have I made a mistake?
I don't feel right in this place
My emotional stats
Read like the share market chart.

I feel like popcorn in a pot
I laugh, I cry, I pray a lot
I wonder whether he likes me?

Am I too care free?
Do I fit in too easily?
I don't feel comfortable
In my own skin.

It's not so much could he love me
For I feel sure he could love me dear
It's more about can I love me
Well, I guess, only time will tell.

First Date

The clock was ticking, I was waiting
To hear your footsteps at my door
So romantic, so debonair
I basked in your adoring flair.

As you entered into my world
I nervously tripped on my words
Awkward glances
Friendly banter.

I said too much, I went on and on
Revealing my heart, opening my soul
It left me feeling vulnerable
Will I regret it tomorrow?

I came out of my shell
Feeling happy and whole
But is that the me that he wants to see.

Throughout the date we reminisced
Over common interests and music
We shared stories of our adventures
Dreams past, present, and future.

Am I 'over the top'?
Was I 'too much'?
Will he re-consider?
And prefer someone else?

I've lived my life as a captive bird
Now the cage is flung open, I'll fly upward
It feels so strange, so alien
That I might fly back in and hide again.
No one 'knows' me

I don't 'know' myself
But I like what I see
It's exciting stuff.

Budding Love

I held your face in my hands
I looked into your eyes
I smiled
I sighed.

My heart felt warm
It pours forth love
A friendship is formed
Of that I was sure.

A love I hope will weather many a storm
It does not demand
It's just comfortable.

It's simple, it's clear
No need to fear
Its intent is pure
It's demure.

I speak some words
They come out wrong
I misconstrue
I confuse.

If I write you a poem
The words will flow
Like a gentle river
It will flood your soul.

I mean no harm
As I hesitate
My heart's been bruised
The wounds go deep.

Accept my embrace
One by one
Moment by moment
As genuine.

There's no hurry
No agenda
No mystery
That's just who I am.

No 'woe is me'
Let's keep it light
Be happy and kind
Friendly and polite.

Cliff Edge of Love

I stand on the cliff face
My toes gripping the edge
I raise my hands to the heavens
My heart is exposed.

The beat of my heart
Pounds like village drums
A deep rumble
An entrancing rhythm.

The wind swirls around me
Urging me on
Then pulling me back
Testing my strength.

A gentle voice whispers to me
As I teeter there
Tentatively balanced
Between past and future.

The suns warmth
Beats down on my heart
Penetrating – burning
Like my lover's words.

I hear his voice
Calling me to him
To come and join him
In the cool valley below.

To bath together
In the cool river of love
And immerge – refreshed – invigorated.

To lay back in his arms
On the soft green grass
That line the bank
Of the river of love.

The voice now teasing me
Dancing in my head
'While it is springtime
Come to me – trust me.'

'Leave the scorching sun
Bitter winter wind
You'll be safe in my love
I promise you.'

With one flex of my toes
Pushed against the cliff edge
My life moves forward
Falling into you.

There's no going back
I leave my past behind
Free falling toward
Your river of love.

The Web of Love

'At any age, falling in love is an enticing web of desire. The threads of the web sparkle in the sunshine of attraction and romantic love, mesmerizing and drawing us closer. As we reach out and touch the web, its sticky thread never let us go.'

Wilted No More

Looking out the small oval-shaped window, Grace watched the city of Melbourne appear through the clouds as the plane descended. She smiled to herself: a new city, a new future, far away from Brisbane. It was her eighteenth birthday, and she had not wasted a second in escaping the chaos of her childhood, leaving her family and a full-time job to pursue her first romance. She was the youngest child, yet the first to leave home. She remembered the gloomy expression on her parents' faces as she had waved goodbye but refused to let their sadness hinder her own bold happiness. She had chosen a location far away from them, far away from their melancholy existence.

The wing flaps extended, and the aircraft dragged and slowed. The wheels touched down on the runway, and with the shudder Grace's attention jolted back to the present moment. Fear and excitement churned in her stomach.

Once the plane had stopped, Grace followed the other passengers along the narrow aisle to the exit and stepped out into her new life. Picking up her pace along the gateway, she entered the arrivals lounge, and spotted Alex amongst the waiting crowd. She ran to him and fell into his arms.

'Welcome to Melbourne,' Alex grinned.

As they drove through Melbourne City toward Alex's family home in Montmorency, he chattered about what he had planned for them to do over the coming weekend. Grace listened in a semi daze, her emotions bouncing around in her mind. There was no going back. She had fallen in love with Melbourne City the same time she had fallen in love with Alex eighteen months earlier. And here she was. Her dream had come true. And yet she was so nervous. She had never lived away from her family home. Now she would have to find somewhere to live and secure full time work as soon as possible.

'Here we are.'

As Alex unloaded Grace's suitcase from the car, his mother, Anne, came out of the house to greet them.

'Relax Grace, you know she doesn't bite.'

Anne smiled as she approached Grace. She was a tall woman, with a shock of short blonde hair.

'Happy birthday, Grace.'

'Thank-you, Mrs. Matthew.'

'I've set up the spare room for you. You're welcome to stay until you get yourself sorted. Come in, I've got a roast cooking in the oven.'

Thank you for reading my book!

If you enjoyed this book, I'd be very grateful if you would leave a short review on Goodreads. Your support really does make a difference. I read all the reviews personally so I can get your feedback and make the book even better.

Thanks again,

Kate Kelsen